game ⇄
changer

ALSO BY MARGARET PETERSON HADDIX

The Always War
Claim to Fame
Palace of Mirrors
Uprising
Double Identity
The House on the Gulf
Escape from Memory
Takeoffs and Landings
Turnabout
Just Ella
Leaving Fishers
Don't You Dare Read This, Mrs. Dunphrey

THE MISSING SERIES
Found
Sent
Sabotaged
Torn
Caught

THE SHADOW CHILDREN SERIES
Among the Hidden
Among the Impostors
Among the Betrayed
Among the Barons
Among the Brave
Among the Enemy
Among the Free

The Girl with 500 Middle Names
Because of Anya
Say What?
Dexter the Tough
Running Out of Time

MARGARET PETERSON
HADDIX

game ⇌

changer

SIMON & SCHUSTER BFYR

New York   London   Toronto   Sydney   New Delhi

SIMON & SCHUSTER BFYR

An imprint of Simon & Schuster Children's Publishing Division
1230 Avenue of the Americas, New York, New York 10020
SIMON & SCHUSTER BFYR is a trademark of Simon & Schuster, Inc.
For information about special discounts for bulk purchases, please contact Simon & Schuster Special Sales at 1-866-506-1949 or
business@simonandschuster.com.
The Simon & Schuster Speakers Bureau can bring authors to your live event. For more information or to book an event, contact the Simon & Schuster Speakers Bureau at 1-866-248-3049 or visit our website at
www.simonspeakers.com.
Book design by Krista Vossen
The text for this book is set in Centennial.
Manufactured in the United States of America
2 4 6 8 10 9 7 5 3 1
Library of Congress Cataloging-in-Publication Data
Haddix, Margaret Peterson.
Game changer / Margaret Peterson Haddix.—1st ed.
p. cm.
Summary: While playing in the championship softball game, star pitcher KT Sutton blacks out and awakes to a changed world where the roles of academics and sports at her middle school have flipped, making talented athletes, such as KT, outcasts and brainy nerds popular.
ISBN 978-0-689-87380-5 (hardcover)
ISBN 978-1-4424-5389-0 (eBook)
[1. Middle schools—Fiction. 2. Schools—Fiction. 3. Space and time—Fiction. 4. Individuality—Fiction. 5. Sports—Fiction.] I. Title.
PZ7.H1164Gam 2012
[Fic] —dc23
2011034707

FIRST
EDITION

For the 1982 Miami Trace High School "In the Know" team,

The 2010 and 2011 Dublin Scioto "In the Know" teams,

The Bishop Hall gang,

The New Year's Eve gang (both those who love

the Name Game and those who hate it)

And, of course, the other two-thirds of

the Triumvirate of Knowledge.

The answer is still "Up."

Prologue

KT Sutton swung her arm in a phantom arc. Her hand released a phantom ball.

The perfect pitch.

In reality KT was sitting in the backseat of her family's SUV. But in her mind she was on the field in the championship game of the Rysdale Invitational, hurling perfect pitch after perfect pitch over the plate, striking out one stunned batter after another.

If you can see it, you can do it.

Her pitching coach's words echoed in her mind, filling her mind. The whole world shrank to those words and KT's imagined perfect pitches.

See it; do it. See it; do it. See it—

"You're not nervous, are you?" her father's voice came from the front seat. "There's no reason to be nervous. You're the best pitcher out there. The scouts will see that."

KT clenched her fists. The imaginary pitcher she was

visualizing in her mind dropped the imaginary ball. Pain shot through her very real muscles. The semifinal game yesterday had been hard-fought and brutal, and KT just hadn't bounced back like she usually did.

"Dad," she said, her voice as cutting as one of her perfect pitches. "Stop it."

"Don't jinx her," Mom advised from the passenger seat.

"Mom," KT said. She gritted her teeth to fight the pain still throbbing in her right shoulder. "Don't talk about jinxes."

"It's just—" Dad shifted in his seat. KT could tell he was trying to catch her eye in the rearview mirror. "This is a really important game. Maybe the most important game of your softball career so far. "

KT bent her neck, avoiding Dad's gaze. Even that movement hurt. She stared at the mitt cradled in her lap, letting her eyes draw comfort from the familiar pattern of the lacings.

"Why don't you let us help you get psyched up?" Dad asked. "Like you used to."

"I'm not eight anymore," KT said.

She remembered how Dad had prepared her for games back then. He'd have her stand at the top of the stairs in their house and yell, "I'm the best pitcher in the world! I'm the best pitcher in the world!" over and over again—"until you believe it," he always said.

At eight she'd believed easily. She'd torn through the Ponytail League so dramatically that three ten-and-under travel teams came recruiting her. She'd heard her father brag once that "My daughter could throw strikes with her eyes closed," so she'd tried it in the next game.

And succeeded.

She'd been eight when she'd written out her goals for life, in lurching little-kid writing:

The University of Arizona will beg me to pitch for them

I will win a gold medal in the Olympics

That list was still tacked up on the bulletin board over her bed at home, right in the center where she could see it every day. Her goals hadn't changed in the least since then, but just so other people understood, she'd added a few clarifications over the years. She could close her eyes and picture the list as it had looked when she'd stared at it that very morning:

The University of Arizona will BEG me to pitch for them. They will give me a full-ride scholarship. I will be their starting pitcher.

I will win a gold medal in the Olympics. I'll start for TEAM USA, too. After I (and 9 million other players) convince the Olympic Committee to bring

softball back! Or, if that doesn't work, at least I'll get a gold in the World Cup!

High-school and college scouts always watched the Rysdale Invitational. Maybe the people who would be Olympic coaches someday did too. KT was only in eighth grade, but everyone said this was when the really important people started paying attention. When they started filling slots on the best high-school teams, the ones that brought together girls from hundreds of miles apart. When they began planning who would get which college scholarship. When they mentally began filling lineups for games that wouldn't be played for years.

This was when KT could start making her dreams come true.

A shiver passed through her that could have been fear, could have been nerves, or could have been another jolt of pain.

KT decided it was just adrenaline. The pure, raw adrenaline that was going to propel her to pitch a perfect game.

In the front seat Mom put a warning hand on Dad's arm.

"Bill," she said soothingly. "KT has a professional psych-up routine now. We paid her pitching coach and her visualization coach a lot of money to work up the best approach for her."

KT heard mumbling beside her—something like, "Should have spent that money on video games."

KT whipped her head to the side and held back a wince at the pain that flowed from that motion. Somehow she'd managed to forget that her younger brother, Max, was in the car too.

Forgetting him, she'd discovered, was the best strategy with Max. But she couldn't stop herself from snarling, "What'd you say?"

Max barely bothered to glance up from his Nintendo DS. He darted his eyes nervously toward Mom and Dad in the front seat and mumbled, "Nothing."

Just looking at Max annoyed KT. How could two kids from the same family be so different? He'd been a cute enough little kid, with wavy blond hair and ears that stuck out in a way that made strangers stop them in the grocery store and gush, "What an adorable little boy!" But now that he was twelve, he'd turned into a pudgy, pasty blob who might as well have had his hands surgically attached to various video and computer games. A human slug, as far as KT was concerned.

Pathetic. Despicable. Disgusting.

"Max, honey, don't bother your sister," Mom said, turning around to fix him with one of her stares. Just from her tone, KT could tell this was probably a continuation of some earlier scolding. The "honey" sounded like a threat. "KT is under enough pressure as it is. We all need to support her as a family."

Thanks a lot, Mom, KT thought. *You're not helping either.*

Max waited until Mom turned back around to face the front. Then he muttered, barely loud enough for even KT to hear, "It's just a *game.* Who cares?"

KT felt the anger blast through her body. *How dare he . . .* She actually welcomed the anger, because it washed over the pain, over the fear, over the nerves.

Use it, she told herself.

She'd done that in plenty of games, drawing on fury over bad plays, bad calls, or bad sportsmanship to make her own game that much sharper. But somehow today she couldn't get quite . . . centered. Without exactly realizing it, she'd gone from cradling her mitt in her lap to cradling her right arm.

It doesn't hurt that much, she told herself. *I'll be fine once I warm up. But . . . there's nothing wrong with buying myself a little insurance.*

Surreptitiously, she sneaked her left hand down into the bag at her feet. She came up with a bottle of Advil. Working one-handed, she popped off the lid and slid two tablets into her mouth, washing them down with a swig from her water bottle.

There, KT thought. *Mom and Dad didn't see, so they won't be asking annoying questions like, "What's wrong? Are you going to be okay to pitch? Are you still going to be in top form? You have to be in top form!" And of course Max wouldn't notice. For once it's good he's a video-game-addicted slug!*

Moments later they pulled into the parking lot of the sports complex. Maybe it was the Advil kicking in; maybe it was just the excitement finally hitting. But KT didn't feel like she needed her psych-up exercises anymore. This was it—the big game. She forgot anger, annoyance, pain, fear, nerves. The green grass of the field spread out before her. In the parking lot the bright gold and blue of her teammates' uniforms glowed as if the sun shone only for them.

My tribe, KT thought. *My home.*

The field was flat enough that she could see straight out to the pitching circle.

Where I belong, KT thought.

Kerri and Bree, two of her teammates, began pumping their fists at KT as soon as they saw her.

"Woo-hoo!" they screamed. "KT's here! Time to dominate!"

They slapped their palms against the side of the SUV, letting the sound accelerate and crescendo. Two other teammates, Makenna and Liz, ran over to join in.

"Dad, stop! Let me out here!" KT demanded.

"Um, okay. Good lu—"

KT was out of the car and slamming the door before he finished the last word. But KT knew what it was, and she didn't need it.

Luck? That's not what wins games. It's talent. Training. Hard work. Skill. It's wanting to win so bad you can taste it.

KT already had that.

It was the top of the fifth inning, and KT's team was behind 3-2.

Coach Mike sent her out to the pitching circle with a slap on the back and three words: "Shut 'em down."

KT had been pitching for Coach Mike for two years. She knew exactly what he was asking for: three strikeouts in a row, nine pitches so dazzling and tricky that three of the best fourteen-year-old batters in the country would swing and miss, swing and miss, swing and miss. Boom, boom, boom. You're out; you're done; your half of the inning is over. It's our turn now, baby.

KT knew that if Coach Mike had been sending out one of the other pitchers, Vanessa, he would have said, "Get back our at-bat." Vanessa liked the drama; she needed that sense of revenge, the suggestion that something that rightfully belonged to her team had been taken away and she needed to take it back.

KT liked keeping things simple.

But as she jogged onto the field, everything behind Coach Mike's words flashed through her mind. He didn't want three strikeouts just because it would be quick. He wanted those strikeouts as psychological warfare. Ten or fifteen minutes from now, when the teams switched sides, he wanted the girls from the other team spreading across the field thinking, *Maybe we're not as good as we thought we were. Maybe we deserve to lose. Maybe we're losers after all.*

And he wanted those strikeouts for KT's sake, to show what she could do. KT didn't know if there were really scouts there or not—Coach Mike had a policy of not talking about things like that until after a game—but a few people in the stands didn't seem to be cheering for either side, and that was always a tip-off. KT had done well in the first four innings, but she'd let two runners get on base. She just hoped the scouts noticed that none of them actually scored. All three of the Cobras' runs had come last inning, when Vanessa was pitching, not KT.

Never mind. KT was back now. She was ready to pitch her best.

KT dug her cleats into the ground, marking her territory. She swung her arm around, loosening it up. It took every ounce of willpower she had not to flinch at the aching protest her arm sent up, but KT managed to keep her expression poker-face smooth. She got into position, and that hurt too.

No pain, no gain, she thought, and hurled the ball toward the catcher's mitt.

The batter swung so hard KT could almost feel the breeze. "Strike one!" the umpire hollered.

When she was batting, KT hated those words. She'd tell herself, *That's nothing. Just a warm-up swing. Give me another one like that and I'll hit it out of the park.*

KT could tell that this batter was telling herself the same thing.

Oh, no, you won't, KT thought, and she threw the next ball.

"Strike two!" the umpire called.

Told you, KT thought.

Two strikes, no balls—it would be easy for a pitcher to get cocky at this point. To start counting her strikeouts before they were pitched, to maybe even look toward the next batter warming up off to the side. But KT's coaches had all but beaten into her brain: *Finish the job. You start celebrating too soon, it's you who's going to be finished.*

So KT allowed herself only one triumphant nod, a quick jerk of her chin down and back up. Out of the corner of her eye she could see Bree over on first base, nodding back. It was like they were connected telepathically, each one thinking, *Don't tell Coach Mike, but we might as well start celebrating now, because we are going to win this thing.*

The batter stepped out of the batter's box, tried a few experimental swings, and stepped back in.

Losing confidence, are we? KT thought. She threw the next ball.

"Strike three!" the umpire cried.

KT could tell he was trying to hide the admiration in his voice. He was supposed to be neutral, after all. But those had been three beautiful pitches. The Cobras were known for their batting. They *never* struck out.

The next batter took her time getting to the plate.

Trying to make me cool down my hot arm? KT thought. *Uh-uh. Not going to happen.*

But the momentary break gave KT a second to feel the throbbing in her arm again.

I thought Advil was supposed to last longer than this, she thought. *Guess I won't be doing any commercials for* them *after I'm in the Olympics.*

The batter was ready now.

So was KT.

The pitch.

The swing.

The umpire's call: "Strike one!"

And again.

"Strike two!"

And again.

"Strike three!"

Nothing to it, KT thought, even as the stands went wild. KT could hear her parents' voices loudest of all, calling out: "KT! KT! KT!"

"Just one more strikeout!" her father yelled.

Coming right up, KT thought.

But she knew those last two batters had been the bottom of the Cobras' lineup—talented girls, probably good enough right now, at fourteen, to star on most varsity high school softball teams in the country. They could probably star on a lot of college teams too. But compared with the rest of the Cobras, they weren't stars. They were inconsequential specks of dust.

The Cobras' star batter was coming up next.

Her name was Chelisha, and she was so famous in softball circles that KT had heard rumors about her even though she lived hundreds of miles away. Supposedly, her father had been a record-breaking baseball player in Cuba; her mother had been an Olympic skier. Supposedly, she'd hit her first home run when she was two.

Chelisha, in batting stance, was a portrait of coiled-up power and menace. She *looked* like a cobra.

Yesterday, watching the Cobras' semifinal game, KT had been in awe of Chelisha's elegance, her grace, her speed— and the three runs she batted in during the second inning, the home run she sent sailing over the fence in the fourth, the triple she scored on in the sixth.

"Wouldn't you love to be the pitcher who struck her out?" Vanessa had whispered to KT.

Oh, yeah, KT thought.

Now was her chance.

Under her batting helmet Chelisha fixed her eyes on KT's—*a trick*, KT thought. *She's trying to rattle me.*

For just an instant a jab of self-doubt pierced KT's brain: *Who am I to strike out the great Chelisha? She's amazing. Maybe I'm not as good a pitcher as I thought. Maybe I've just been lucky. Maybe, underneath it all, I'm just a loser.*

Whoa. Chelisha was *good*. And all she was doing was standing there.

Oh, no, you don't, KT thought, narrowing her eyes right back at Chelisha. *Who are you to think you can get a hit off the great KT? I just struck out two of your teammates, and now I'm going to strike out you!*

KT threw the first pitch.

It was a little . . . erratic. KT had been working so hard to block out the pain radiating through her body that maybe she was ignoring other signals too. Like where her hand was when she let go of the ball.

The ball dipped, then rose, then dipped again. The last time KT had pitched so gracelessly was her first game in the Ponytail League, six years earlier. But the ball crossed the plate in the strike zone.

And—it wasn't what Chelisha was expecting. She swung a second too late, a millimeter too high.

"Strike one!" the umpire called.

So there! KT thought. *Even when I mess up I'm great!*

But she didn't have to turn her head to feel Coach Mike glaring at her. She knew exactly what he was thinking: *There'll be no more of that. Nobody can win with pitches like that. Can you get your act back together, or should I take you out?*

"It's back together," KT whispered to herself.

She hoped.

She got back into position, her own version of a coiled cobra ready to strike. Or—ready to throw a strike. Her entire being was focused on that one action: every nerve, every muscle, every tendon, every ligament, every brain cell. She whipped her arm around and—boom!

The ball lay in the catcher's mitt.

Chelisha hadn't even tried for it.

"Strike two!" the umpire called.

Who's bad now? KT's eyes asked Chelisha.

Chelisha was a cool customer. She yawned.

Just waiting for something worth hitting, her eyes said

back to KT. *You going to throw something I can respect or am I going to have to make do with garbage like that?*

Respect this, KT thought back at her.

She got back into pitching position. She could feel her teammates behind her, and knew without looking that they were in position too. She knew they were ready for anything, but hoping for two things at the same time. Deep in their hearts they were wishing for KT to throw another strike, because they could be generous like that, and they knew how happy she would be to strike out Chelisha. But, just as deep in their hearts, all of them were also wishing that Chelisha's bat would connect with the ball and send it soaring straight into a glove—their own. Because every girl wanted to be the hero. You didn't practice ten or twenty hours a week just to stand on a field and do nothing.

Sorry, girls, KT thought. *Maybe next time. This one's mine.*

She hurled the ball toward the plate.

The pitch was just a bit outside the strike zone, but maybe Chelisha wasn't as cool as she pretended. She reached for it. She jerked her bat around to slam the ball down toward the ground. The ball bounced once, speeding back toward the pitching circle. It was just to KT's right.

KT could see in her mind's eye exactly what would happen if she didn't stop that ball. The third baseman, Kerri, would scoop it up a split second too late, and fire it toward Bree, on first, another split second too late—and Chelisha would already be on base.

KT had to get that ball.

It was awkward, leaping sideways and at the same time reaching up and to the right with her gloved left hand. But

KT had done this exact move a million times in practices and other games. It was automatic for her, her muscles working in sync practically before her brain could process, *That ball's mine. Grab it!*

KT reached higher, higher, higher. The ball seemed rocket-powered, headed for outer space. Definitely beyond KT's glove.

No! screamed through KT's mind. *I'm stopping it!*

She made her arm stretch farther. The ball slammed against the lacing at the top of the glove, and for a fraction of a second it felt like the ball itself was trying to decide: *Stay here or keep flying on?*

KT jerked her right hand over the ball, a risky move because she didn't have the glove firmly in place, solidly behind it. But the gamble worked. She squeezed her hand tight, and the ball was right there, firm against her palm. She whipped around and fired the ball toward Bree on first base.

Something happened during that throw. Her arm flailed out of control. A wave of pain crashed through her body—too big to ignore, too overwhelming to fight. KT couldn't even surrender, because the pain didn't ask her to surrender. It just took over.

The pain slammed her to the ground. Darkness sagged over her vision; a buzzing took over her ears. But her brain gasped out one more thought before it, too, shut down:

Where'd I throw that ball?

Chapter One

KT fought against waking up.

It'll hurt, she thought. *Can't face it . . . can't . . . can't . . .*

As lullabies went, this one sucked. Each "can't" forced her closer and closer to consciousness, as inevitably as a swimmer surfacing after a dive.

Stubbornly, she kept her eyes squeezed shut. She held her body perfectly still.

Can't look, she thought. *Can't move. Can't call the pain to me.*

She had a vague sense that she might be in a hospital, might be in traction, might be in one of those full-body casts where nothing showed but the patient's eyes. If she let herself listen, she was fairly certain that she'd hear beeping monitors, doctors' and nurses' regretful voices, maybe even her own parents' sobbing.

She didn't want to let herself listen.

Then, as so often happened, she heard Coach Mike's voice in her mind.

There's no room for cowards on a softball team, it was saying.

KT forced herself to open her eyes.

And—she grinned.

She wasn't in a hospital room. There was no traction, no cast; there were no monitors, no doctors or nurses. She was simply in her own bed at home, the morning light streaming in through the windows so blindingly that she couldn't see through it.

Perfect softball weather, she thought, as she did any time it was sunny.

Automatically, she rolled over to squint at the clock on her nightstand. It said 7:23, and a little M–F glowed red beside the numbers, meaning that her usual weekday alarm was on.

School day, KT thought, relaxing muscles she hadn't quite realized were tense. *Just an ordinary school day.*

She still had seven minutes before her alarm went off, so she reached for the softball nestled on the nightstand beside the clock. She flipped over onto her back and tossed the ball up into the air a few times, letting gravity bring it back to her again and again and again.

This was her favorite way to wake up.

I'm KT Sutton, pitcher, she thought. *There's nothing else to say.*

She savored the pull of her muscles, the smack of the ball against her bare palm. She tightened her grip around the ball, as if ready to throw it as hard as she could, and her hand and arm and shoulder felt absolutely fine. She flexed her wrists, her ankles, her neck. Not a single nerve ending complained.

This was miraculous. KT couldn't remember the last time

she hadn't had some part of her body aching at least a little—a pulled muscle, a shin splint, a tender bruise growing on her leg from sliding into base. She sat up on the edge of her bed, and still nothing hurt.

See? She told herself. *I'm fine. Better than ever. Nothing's wrong at all. Nothing happened last night except . . .*

The Rysdale Invitational.

KT actually gasped out loud. How could she have forgotten? Last night had been the Rysdale Invitational championship game—the game she'd been longing to play for the past three years, the game that could help determine her high-school and college career, and maybe even her post-college career too. And what had happened?

She remembered the first four innings. She remembered striking out the first two batters in the fifth inning. She remembered pitching to the mighty Chelisha. Strike one. Strike two. Chelisha swinging for the third pitch, the ball bouncing, KT catching it. And then . . .

KT's memory shut down.

Well, of course I threw the ball to first, KT thought. *Of course.*

Why couldn't she remember that throw? Why couldn't she remember anything that happened after that throw? Why did her memory keep backing away every time she tried to think about it?

Don't worry about any of that, she told herself. *Who won? How'd we do in the rest of the game? How'd I do?*

She reached for her iPod from behind the alarm clock. She checked the clock again. She still had four minutes. Plenty of time to log on to the Rysdale Invitational website, find out the final score. If she was lucky, they'd have a description of the championship game posted too.

She logged on to the Internet and swiped through choices on the iPod screen. For some reason, the shortcut to that site was missing, so she had to type out each letter individually: www.rysdaleinvitational.org.

"Sorry, we couldn't find www.rysdaleinvitational.org" appeared on the screen.

That was weird. Had KT misspelled something? Was it ".com" or ".net" or something like that? She tried all the other possibilities she could think of.

Nothing.

The alarm on her clock went off—a deep, disturbing buzz. KT jumped.

Stop it, she told herself. *You set that alarm yourself. Nothing's wrong. Do you hear me? Nothing's wrong.*

She shut off the alarm and dropped the iPod back onto the nightstand. KT had patience for pitching and pitching and pitching, and listening to instructions to move her foot a millimeter to the left or slide her thumb a millimeter to the right. She didn't have patience with iPods or computers or other electronics if they didn't do what she wanted them to do instantly so she could get back to things she really cared about.

Duh, KT thought. *Just go see if you have the winner's trophy or the runner-up trophy.*

She pulled a warm-up jacket and pants over her T-shirt and shorts and dashed out of her room.

KT's trophies—dozens and dozens of them, maybe even hundreds—were all displayed downstairs on a family-room bookshelf that her parents lovingly referred to as "the shrine." It was actually silly to call it a bookshelf, since it contained no books. The trophies and medals and team pictures had completely taken over. Anytime KT came home with a new trophy, it got the prime position on the shelf, and then a day or so later her dad would prop up a picture beside it of KT holding the trophy at the end of the game: tired, sweaty, sometimes covered in mud and bruises, but always grinning triumphantly.

It'll be the championship trophy, KT told herself as she raced down the stairs. *It's got to be. We had to have gotten Chelisha out at first. We had to have come back and gotten at least two more runs . . .*

KT leaped past the last three stairs and spun around the corner into the family room. She saw the vast wooden structure of the shrine. She turned her head, zeroing in on the center shelf, the position of honor. She saw . . .

Nothing.

It wasn't just that there was no Rysdale Invitational championship or runner-up trophy on the center shelf. There was nothing there at all. The shelf was completely bare. KT took a step back, her gaze taking in the entire structure.

All the shelves were empty. All of KT's trophies were gone.

KT let out a sound that might have been a whimper.

Mom's head appeared over the back of the couch.

"Where . . . th-the trophies . . . ," KT managed to stammer.

"What? Oh—I'm dusting," Mom said. She held up something that must have been a trophy, enswathed in a huge dust cloth. Mom bent down again, her head disappearing behind the couch once more.

KT sagged against the wall in relief. Of course Mom was

just dusting. KT had seen her do this many times: moving all the trophies and medals and pictures down to the floor, wiping down the shelves, then running the cloth over each individual trophy before placing it back in its exact right spot.

KT waited for Mom to bob back up. Maybe Mom would say something like, "Great game last night!" and then KT could say, "What was your favorite part?" And just by saying "uh-huh" and "you think so?" a few times, KT could get Mom to tell her everything.

Mom and Dad *loved* reliving KT's games.

Mom didn't reappear. Should KT just say, "Hey, let me see last night's trophy again?" Could she do that without making Mom suspicious?

Mom's phone rang. It wasn't her usual ring tone—"Take Me Out to the Ball Game"—but some chant KT had never heard before. She couldn't quite make out the words.

"Hello?" Mom said, after standing up and pulling the phone out of her pocket. She twisted side to side, as if her back was sore from bending over dusting.

Maybe it would be Grandma and Grandpa, and Mom would tell them the whole story of how the game had gone last night. Maybe it would be the mother of one of KT's teammates, and KT could figure out from the conversation whether the two moms thought KT had earned her choice of spots on the best high-school club teams, or if KT had hurt her chances.

"Oh, yeah, it's a big one," Mom said.

That sounded promising.

"Yes, we're very proud of our little Max," Mom went on.

Max? KT thought. *Liar. Why would you be proud of him?*

Amazingly, it seemed that the entire conversation was going to be about Max.

"Yes, yes, he's been working very hard. . . . Yes, everyone says his chances are good. . . . Yes, that's just what my husband and I think . . . ," Mom was saying.

KT started tuning out the Max talk. But she decided she could inch closer to the couch. All she needed was one glimpse of the Rysdale Invitational trophy on the floor behind the couch and she'd at least know if her team had won or lost. Then maybe she could check Facebook for more details.

Even as she said, "Uh-huh, uh-huh," into the phone, Mom screwed up her face and shook her head at KT. Mom made a shooing motion with her free hand.

"Breakfast," she half mouthed, half whispered to KT.

KT froze. Something weird was going on. Mom did not yammer on and on about Max and just shoo KT away. Mom liked to sit with KT while she was eating breakfast. They'd reminisce about the most recent game or sync plans for which teammates' moms were driving the carpool to practice when. Or they'd just daydream together about the big games KT would play in the future. Usually KT was the one who wanted to shoo *Mom* away.

"But—," KT started to say.

Mom's head-shaking became even more stern.

"Go on," she said, pointing toward the kitchen. She went back to her phone conversation. "I'm sorry. My daughter just interrupted me. What were you saying?"

KT backed away.

Interrupted? she thought resentfully. *Didn't that phone call interrupt me and Mom?*

KT felt so strange—maybe breakfast would be a good idea. Could a bowl of Wheaties restore her memory of last night's game?

In the kitchen KT found that Dad had left the local suburban newspaper in a pile on the table. KT fell on it eagerly. The newspaper wasn't very good about covering softball, but the Rysdale Invitational was *huge*. And it was the only big tournament of its kind in the area. The fact that a local team had won—if KT's team really had won—was almost like someone winning the Olympics in her hometown.

It should be front-page news, KT thought.

That was probably too much to hope for—yep, nothing about softball on the front page. KT shuffled through the pages, looking for the sports section.

There wasn't a sports section.

Maybe there was a story, maybe even a picture, and Dad took the whole section to work to show to his coworkers, KT thought.

She flipped through the pages once more, just to be sure, and a thick section labeled ACADEMICS fell out. Its front page was covered with four huge stories about a new chemistry professor starting at the local university. There were three different pictures of the professor, posed with a Bunsen burner, a rack of test tubes, and a pair of safety goggles.

Yeah, and this is why no one reads newspapers anymore, KT thought, dropping the whole stack back onto the table.

But her stomach felt too queasy all of a sudden for cereal and milk. She grabbed an energy bar and, chewing it, went back to her own room.

Facebook, she told herself. *Should have tried that in the first place.*

Vanessa, the backup pitcher on KT's team, loved Facebook. Coach Mike had accused her once of trying to post to it between pitches.

"You don't see KT doing anything like that, do you?" Coach Mike had asked. "You want to be as good as KT, you're going to have to learn how to concentrate like KT."

KT had glowed over those words. She'd memorized them, and replayed them in her mind again and again and again.

But right now she hoped that Vanessa hadn't followed Coach Mike's advice too completely. She had to find out how the game had turned out.

KT crammed the last of the energy bar into her mouth and grabbed her iPod from the nightstand once more. She sat down on the bed and opened Facebook.

Some kid she barely knew from school was asking how she did on some test.

Some other kid from school was asking about some other test.

Oh, who cares? KT thought impatiently.

She decided to go straight to Vanessa's wall. She typed in Vanessa's name, and her profile picture came up—not the one of Vanessa in batting stance that she usually used, but Vanessa in some nerdy-looking argyle sweater vest and nerdy-looking glasses.

Must be Dress Like a Nerd Day on Facebook, KT thought. *Yeah, Vanessa, think how much pitching practice you could have gotten in while you were posing for and posting that stupid picture.*

She hit Vanessa's link and a question came up:

"Send Vanessa Oglivy a friend request?"

"I'm already Vanessa's friend," she muttered to the iPod.

Re-friending Vanessa was too annoying to deal with right now, so she tried Kerri's Facebook page instead.

"Send Kerri Riverton a friend request?" the iPod asked.

"You have got to be kidding," KT muttered.

KT tried Bree. She tried the rest of the infield players, the entire outfield.

According to Facebook, KT wasn't friends with a single one of them.

Great. This would be the day that Facebook messes up, KT thought. She dropped the iPod and picked up her cell phone instead.

"What's your favorite memory of last night's game? Pls share," she typed into the text-message window. That would do it. She'd simply text this to every member of the team at once, and the information would come rolling in. Everyone would think it was a little strange, but KT was beyond caring about that right now. She clicked over to her address book, looking for the group designation for the entire team.

It wasn't there.

In fact, all her team members' individual numbers were missing too. So was most of KT's address book—just about every number except the ones for Mom, Dad, Max, and a few random people from school.

KT dropped her phone, too.

"Mom," she called. She gathered complaints in her head, trying to figure out which to unleash first: *Facebook is broken and my cell phone is messed up and the Rysdale Invitational website is down and the sports section of the paper is missing and why'd you pick today to dust my trophies?*

She could already hear Mom's footsteps on the stairs. Belatedly, some sense of caution swam over KT. *Can't let Mom know I don't remember what happened at the game last night. Can't let her think there's anything wrong with me. She might not let me go to softball practice this afternoon.*

"KT, whatever it is, just hold on a minute," Mom called from out in the hall. "I have to wake up Max."

Yeah, that lazy bum was probably up half the night playing video games, KT thought scornfully. *Of course you have to wake him up.*

But the irritated tone in Mom's voice stung. The way Mom sounded, you'd think KT was some annoying little brat calling out "Mommy, Mommy, Mommy!" over nothing. Not a star pitcher who'd maybe (probably?) won the Rysdale Invitational last night.

KT sat perfectly still, straining her ears to listen.

Mom's footsteps went into Max's room.

"Good morning!" Mom exclaimed, and the hallway that joined KT's and Max's rooms grew brighter. Mom must have just opened Max's curtains.

Lazybones can't even do that for himself, KT thought.

"Rise and shine!" Mom was saying to Max. Her voice brimmed with excitement, with pride. "It's your big day!"

Big day? For Max? What? KT thought.

Of all the strange things that had happened this morning, this was the strangest of all. Something was really, really wrong.

Mom had said exactly those same words, in exactly that same way, to KT yesterday.

So why was she saying them to Max today?

Chapter TwO

KT bolted.

"Mom, I'm ready for school early," she called in the direction of Max's room, even as she grabbed shoes and socks and dashed for the door. "I'm not going to wait for the bus. I'm going to jog over there now."

It was instinct on KT's part. Faced with a problem, any problem, she didn't sit around thinking and deliberating and pondering and hemming and hawing and wondering about a possible solution. She *moved.*

"Our daughter's a girl of action," she'd heard Dad brag about her once.

It might have been after that game where the second baseman fell and broke her arm during an important play, so KT had had to carry the ball to base, rather than throwing it. She'd arrived a split second before the runner. She'd been the hero of the game.

Remembering that moment always gave KT a little jolt of

pride. But right now it wasn't enough, not when she felt so jittery and off-kilter, not when everything that had happened this morning had been so strange and wrong. Not when she had such a huge, gaping hole in her memory of the Rysdale Invitational.

To counter all that, KT had to run.

KT was just escaping from her room when Mom cut her off in the hallway.

"You're jogging to school?" Mom asked. "Really? Oh, KT, do you have to?"

Mom's voice sagged under the weight of—was that disapproval? Disappointment? Dismay?

KT was not used to Mom talking to her like that. KT had jogged to school before—it was only a mile and a half through the neighborhood. Jogging or running or even just walking to school was a good way to get some exercise before a dreary day of sitting through boring classes.

KT had even heard Mom brag about it.

"Our KT has so much self-discipline," she told people. "She's so motivated, she gets up early to jog to school!"

She made it sound like KT climbed Mount Everest every day before breakfast.

So why was Mom sighing now?

"Mom," KT protested. "I want to."

"Yeah, I know," Mom said, letting out another sigh. She seemed to be trying to smile at KT. Since when did it take so much effort? She awkwardly patted KT's shoulder. "You are who you are, I guess."

Weird, weird, weird.

Those words sang in KT's mind as she sprinted down the

stairs. She wanted to dart into the family room to look for the Rysdale Invitational trophy once again. But Mom was still watching her from the top of the stairs.

Just get out the door, KT told herself. *Just get to school. You can go online during homeroom. The Internet has to be fixed by then. The Rysdale website will be back up. So will all your Facebook friends.*

As always, running soothed her. The rhythmic slap of her soles against the sidewalk was as reassuring as her own pulse. She was halfway to school before she realized that she'd forgotten her iPod, forgotten her phone, even forgotten her backpack.

Never mind, she thought. *Who needs the iPod and phone if they're broken? And if there's any homework due, I can copy somebody else's or do it during class.*

The school had gone to some new system where homework didn't count for much, so even the teachers didn't take it very seriously anymore.

Usually when KT ran to school, she saw plenty of other joggers or walkers in the neighborhood—adults trying to burn off a few calories before they sat at desk jobs all day. Even if she didn't know them, they always gave a friendly wave or nod. Once two moms pushing strollers had yelled out, "You go, girl!" as KT ran past, and KT had heard them behind her explaining to a third mother, "That's that Sutton girl. She's some amazing pitcher. We're going to be able to say we knew her when."

That was another memory KT savored.

But today the whole rest of the neighborhood seemed to have been struck by an attack of Max-style laziness. KT didn't see a single other person out on the sidewalk, just cars driving past and . . .

Was that person pointing at me? KT wondered as yet another car flashed by. *Pointing and—laughing? Why?*

It didn't make sense. Her eyes must have been playing tricks on her.

Still, she lost some of her running-induced calm as she got closer and closer to school. Brecksville Middle School North was a fairly new building, with sprawling wings and soaring rooflines. But somehow its angles seemed wrong today, like one of those LEGO kits Max put together backward when he was little.

Now I know I'm just imagining things, KT told herself. How could the building have changed over the weekend?

She stepped up to a clump of other students waiting outside the front door. None of them were her close friends, but she knew several of them: Cassandra from her language-arts class, Spencer from gym, a few sixth graders who'd told her way back during orientation in the fall how much they wanted to try out for softball. So she was surprised no one even said hi.

"Hey," KT said, kind of generally addressing the whole crowd.

Nobody answered. Cassandra and Spencer both looked up and then, without quite meeting KT's eyes, moved away from her. The rest of the crowd seemed to shift away from her too.

What's that all about? KT wondered.

KT realized that she'd been so rattled leaving home that she'd forgotten to brush or comb her hair.

Well, if that's the problem, who needs any of these people?

KT thought. Still, she stepped slightly away from the group, flipped her head down, and pulled all her hair into one hand-ful. She circled it with a rubber band out of her pocket, and flipped the resulting ponytail back. It made a satisfying slap against her shoulders.

"Does this look any better?" KT asked, aiming the question at the group as a whole. She shrugged. "Not that there's a whole lot I can do with this hair."

It was true. KT's hair was bushy and barely manageable even under the best of circumstances. And it was a boring color—light brown.

KT distinctly saw Cassandra roll her eyes. Two of the sixth graders started whispering to each other.

Probably doesn't have anything to do with me, KT told herself.

But she couldn't quite shake the feeling that it did.

I didn't run far enough or hard enough to actually sweat, so I know I don't stink, KT thought. *And, yeah, I forgot to change out of the T-shirt I slept in, but I've got a nice running suit on over it. Lots of kids wear sweats or running suits to school. It's practically the school uniform. Even for kids who aren't athletes.*

But now that she thought about it, there was something a little off about the clothes the other kids were wearing. Spencer had on what seemed to be a perfectly ordinary T-shirt, but instead of saying NIKE or REEBOK or CHIEFTAINS SOCCER, it was covered with math formulas and the words IT ALL ADDS UP. Cassandra was wearing an oversized T-shirt over what looked like yoga pants. But both were covered with huge pictures of William Shakespeare, including a particularly large view of him on her rear. And one of the sixth graders had on a T-shirt that said TEXAS INSTRUMENTS ROCKS.

Texas Instruments? Didn't they make calculators?

Ooooh. KT finally figured it out. *That Dress Like a Nerd thing wasn't just on Facebook. Or the school got the idea from Facebook to do Dress Like a Nerd for Spirit Week.*

Probably the school had sent out some reminder that morning, and KT hadn't seen it because her phone and Facebook were messed up.

The bell rang inside the building, and the door clicked open. KT joined the crowd surging forward. She angled across the entryway toward the school's trophy case. KT was pretty sure the school had put it there on purpose, so any visiting team would get the message right away: *Don't go thinking you could beat us!* Normally, it annoyed KT that the boys' trophies—football and basketball, even wrestling and soccer—were bigger and displayed more prominently than the girls'. But she still liked walking past the trophy case every morning.

Like someone rubbing a lucky coin, she always looked first at the trophy that she herself had had a part in winning last year on the seventh-grade softball team. Then she always looked to the back of the case, where the sports jerseys of the most amazing athletes in Brecksville North history had been retired. Playing on the school team was kind of like going back to preschool after the level of play on her club team. Still, KT harbored a secret dream, one that was more immediate than her main goals of getting a full-ride scholarship to play for the University of Arizona and then winning gold in the Olympics. By the end of this school year, KT

vowed that her own Brecksville North jersey—SUTTON 32—
would hang right up there with Will Stern's baseball jersey
from 2004, Haley Blake's volleyball jersey from 1999, and
Roger Gonzalez's football jersey from 1996. If she pitched
no-hitters every single game of the Brecksville North regular
season, that would do it, wouldn't it?

KT reached the front of the trophy case, and looked down
toward the right corner. Just as she caught the first glimpse
of gold, someone jostled against her, knocking her sideways.

"Hey! Watch it!" KT protested, whipping her head around.
She wanted to say, *Valuable pitching arm here, you know?
The softball team's depending on me!*

But the words froze on her tongue. Because her head was
angled just right to see Will Stern's, Haley Blake's, and Roger
Gonzalez's jerseys. And they weren't there.

Instead, wooden desks hung suspended above the trophies. They were odd, ancient-looking contraptions, with
names engraved on them in gold: DORCAS IMOGENE SMITHERS,
HERBERT STANLEY GOTTLIEB, VIRGIL WALDEMAR VARDEN, EDNA
CORNELIA MEHTA . . .

Who are those people? KT wondered. *And who cares?*

Chapter Thr3e

KT fled to homeroom.

Must find computer, KT thought. *Must see Rysdale Invitational website. Must . . . must . . .*

She stopped and pressed herself against the wall for a moment. She seemed to be having trouble walking and thinking at the same time.

Must make everything normal again.

That was it. That was what she wanted.

She didn't understand how it all fit, but she just knew that if she found out how the Rysdale Invitational championship game had ended last night, everything else would fall into place. Even if the news on the Rysdale website was bad— even if KT's team had lost—she was convinced that knowing would fix everything.

She burst into homeroom with the words "Mrs. Whitbourne, can I use a computer, please?" poised on her lips. Then she stopped, right in the doorway, so abruptly that four other kids slammed into her back.

There weren't any computers in the homeroom classroom.

There weren't any *desks*.

The room had been transformed into a vast, open space, its floor covered with the same kind of blue, foamy mats the phys ed teacher used for gymnastics units.

"Come on, kids, enough with the standing around. You know the drill. Stretches, everyone," the teacher, Mrs. Whitbourne, hollered from the front of the room.

The other kids, grumbling, slid down to the floor. KT watched, confused. She told herself to go into the same kind of crisis management mode she used in risky moments on the softball diamond. Coach Mike had taught her the strategy:

"You don't need to process every piece of information around you. Does it matter that the sky is blue? No. Does it matter it that you didn't get as much playing time in the last inning as you thought you deserved? No. Does it matter that your boyfriend came to watch you play for the very first time?" That one had drawn a laugh from all the girls, and made Coach Mike shake his head even more emphatically. "That doesn't matter either—unless it makes you play better. In which case, yeah, remember that Loverboy Romeo is sitting in the stands. But don't let him distract you. Don't pay attention to anything that doesn't matter. Be a softball-playing machine!"

It didn't matter that KT couldn't figure out what was going on in homeroom. It didn't matter that she couldn't figure out any of the other oddities that had occurred this morning. All that mattered was finding out what had happened in the championship game yesterday.

She walked toward Mrs. Whitbourne.

"Mrs. Whitbourne, may I—," she began.

"No, KT," the teacher interrupted. "You may not."

"But I haven't even said what I—"

Mrs. Whitbourne tucked her clipboard under her arm and ticked off possibilities on her fingers.

"You may not do a more advanced stretching routine than the rest of the class. You may not demonstrate that you might be better at those particular stretching routines than *moi*, your teacher. You may not do anything except get down on that mat and stretch, exactly like I tell you to, exactly like every single other student in this class." Mrs. Whitbourne was practically eyeball to eyeball with KT. "Got it?"

Six years of dealing with high-strung, championship-seeking softball coaches had taught KT that there were certain times when it wasn't wise to argue with grown-ups.

Now appeared to be one of them.

"Yes, ma'am," KT said.

She slid down to the mat and obediently stretched her arms toward her toes, just like all the other students.

But Mrs. Whitbourne couldn't control the thoughts stretching through KT's mind. What if Mrs. Whitbourne's hissy fit wasn't just a fluke, just a teacher upset that it was Monday? What if it was something else? What if KT needed to pay attention to what Mrs. Whitbourne had said?

Why does she act like those are all things that I've done before? KT wondered. *We've never stretched in homeroom before! We always just sit at our desks and listen to boring morning announcements and then go to class. And—Mrs. Whitbourne likes me! At least—I thought she did. She used to play softball herself, so she always likes hearing about my games! She lets me come in late and doesn't even count me tardy!*

The next time KT dipped toward the ground she dared to turn her head a little to the right and whisper to the girl beside her, "What was that all about? What's wrong with Mrs. Whitbourne? And why are we doing stretches? What happened to all the computers and desks?"

The girl, Maria, let out an exasperated snort. She didn't answer KT, but the next time Maria dipped in the other direction, KT heard her tell the girl on the other side of her, "Don't you love it when teachers see through those teacher's-pet routines?"

Teacher's pet? KT thought indignantly. *I'm not a teacher's pet!*

"People! Your form is awful!" Mrs. Whitbourne called from the front of the room. She tapped a finger impatiently against her clipboard. "You do this wrong, you're going to get hurt. Look at . . ." She sighed. "Look at KT. She's the only one doing it entirely correctly. KT, would you demonstrate?"

"Uh, sure," KT said. She made sure her left foot was tucked against her rear, and stretched her arms toward her right shoe. She inched down slowly, just like she'd learned in softball. "Like this?"

"Naturally," Mrs. Whitbourne said, tossing her head scornfully. She was an older woman with short, gray hair—her hair didn't even move. "Okay, people, every single one of you should be doing exactly what KT's doing. Now get to it!"

Maria, the girl beside KT, dipped down alongside her and hissed, "Show-off!"

"But—she asked me to," KT muttered back.

"Hmph," Maria snorted contemptuously.

What's her beef? KT wondered.

Dimly she remembered that Maria had tried out for the school softball team last year, in seventh grade, and had been cut in the first round. She hadn't even bothered trying out this year, so KT figured she didn't really care.

But was Maria still holding a grudge from last year? Was she jealous that KT was the star pitcher and Maria wasn't even good enough to make a seventh-grade team?

KT had been sitting next to Maria in homeroom all year. They didn't usually say much to each other beyond "Hey" and "What's up?" But Maria had never acted jealous before. Why was she so bitter now?

And why were the other kids around them nodding and glaring at KT, like they *all* agreed with Maria?

The bell rang, signaling that it was time for everyone to go to first period.

Not me, KT thought. *At least—not yet.*

She darted out of the classroom and around the corner. She wasn't going to take the risk that her first-period teacher, Mr. Huck, wouldn't let her use a computer either. She was taking matters into her own hand. She'd sneak into the library, check out the Rysdale Invitational website on the computer there, and *then* go to first period.

She turned a second corner. Past the lockers and then . . . KT stopped.

Wait—this isn't the way to the library. It's . . .

She backtracked, almost completely back to homeroom. Start over. Left, then right, then . . .

She'd ended up in the wrong hallway again.

"KT?" a voice called behind her. "Is everything okay?"

KT hesitated. She squinted at the walls around her, willing the doorways and cut-throughs and classrooms to unscramble and reassemble and look familiar again. She'd been going to Brecksville North for three years. How could she have done what sixth graders always feared on their very first day?

She'd gotten completely lost in her own school.

Chapter F0ur

"KT?" the voice behind her said again.

KT whirled around. This nightmare of a morning instantly got worse: It was Mr. Huck, her social-studies teacher. The one whose class she was skipping.

She tried putting on her game face.

"Uh, hey, Mr. Huck," she said brightly, with what she hoped was an innocent-looking smile. "I know I'm late to first period, but—"

Mr. Huck gave her a light, conspiratorial punch on the arm.

"Well, no, technically you're not late yet," he said. The bell rang in the emptying hallway around them. Doors slammed; the hallway fell silent. Now it was just Mr. Huck, KT, and the cinder-block walls.

"*Now* you're late," Mr. Huck said. "But I am too, so I won't tell if you don't."

Mr. Huck had never been quite this . . . friendly before. He was an okay guy, but most of the time in his class KT had the sense that he was just waiting for the school day to end so he could get to what he really loved: coaching the boys' lacrosse team.

KT could respect that. She felt the same way about getting through school to get to softball.

But it didn't make social-studies class very interesting.

"I wanted to talk to you anyhow," Mr. Huck said. He leaned against the wall, as if trying to make their conversation even more private.

They were already standing close together in a deserted hallway.

Is he hitting on me? KT thought with a mix of amazement and disgust. She knew several girls who had crushes on Mr. Huck, because he was kind of good-looking, and it hadn't been that long since he'd been a student at Brecksville North himself. But he was probably twice her age.

KT thought the girls who got crushes on teachers were stupid.

"*Are* you okay?" Mr. Huck asked, his eyebrows wrinkling into worried-looking wedges.

KT forgot her suspicions about him hitting on her. This was more like . . . like he really respected her.

"Nobody's giving you a hard time about that e-mail, are they?" Mr. Huck asked.

E-mail? KT thought. *What e-mail?*

"Um," KT said.

Mr. Huck lowered his voice.

"It's all right," he said. "Mr. Arnold showed it to me in confidence."

Mr. Arnold was the principal.

"He did?" KT said, because she had to say something.

"Yes," Mr. Huck said. He clenched his hand and turned his wrist like someone swinging a pretend lacrosse stick. KT thought she understood the motion, because she always flicked her wrist like she was throwing a pretend softball any time she got stuck in an awkward conversation.

In fact she was doing that right now.

"Why?" KT asked. The word came out more forcefully than she meant it to. She wished Mr. Huck could tell her why Maria had called her a show-off, why Mrs. Whitbourne had been so mean, why they'd done stretches in homeroom, why Facebook and her cell phone and the Rysdale website were messed up, why Mom had acted so weird—and most of all why KT couldn't remember anything after the start of the fifth inning of the championship game yesterday.

And, of course, how the game had ended.

"Let's just say, I am very sympathetic to your viewpoint," Mr. Huck said. "But you came on kind of strong in your accusations, and Mr. Arnold was a little offended—he was quite the chemistry standout, in his day."

Chemistry? KT thought. *What's that got to do with anything?*

"I told Mr. Arnold I remember feeling just like you do when I was in middle school," Mr. Huck said. He gave a sad chuckle. "Not that I was ever brave enough to call anyone out, like you did. Certainly not the school administration and all the coaches!"

Administration? Coaches? What was he talking about?

KT couldn't ask. Asking would be like admitting she'd suddenly forgotten how to find the library in the school she'd been attending the past three years. Or like admitting that she'd forgotten an entire chunk of her life yesterday.

Or—if he's talking about some e-mail I supposedly sent Mr. Arnold, did I maybe forget more than the last half of yesterday? Did I forget something that happened last week, too?

KT remembered last week. She'd had intense softball practice every day.

"Mr. Huck," KT said firmly. "I think you have me mixed up with somebody else."

Mr. Huck frowned and shook his head.

"Don't do that," he said. "We can be honest here. This school does have its priorities mixed up sometimes, and it's the talented students like you who get hurt. It's a crying shame we eliminated the gifted program in those budget cuts a few years back. We do have to gear the education system to the most basic level, to try to make sure everyone passes the state tests at the end of the year. I know that makes everything boring for students like you, who want to soar above the crowd, and . . ."

Now KT *knew* Mr. Huck had her confused with someone else. Nobody had ever accused her of being a talented student before, or of belonging in a gifted program. She was usually on the honor roll, but that was mostly just because they made it easy for anyone to be on the honor roll. If you did badly on a test, there was always a chance to retake it, or do extra credit, or find some other way to get your grades up.

KT zoned out a little, because Mr. Huck was going on and on about how "the school really doesn't mean to clip your wings" and "part of it's just the nature of middle school and middle school students" and "I promise you, it'll get better in high school. Or at least by college. You'll find your peer group eventually, people who care as much as you do about school-work . . ."

He's whacked, KT thought. *A total nut job.*

She'd heard teachers complain, "You guys are going to send me into a nervous breakdown!" But she never thought she'd actually witness it.

She started inching away from him.

"Uh, Mr. Huck, don't you think we should go to class?" she asked. "Everybody's going to be wondering where you are."

"It's okay—I told them to get started without me," Mr. Huck said. He put his hand on KT's arm. "Look, I know this is an uncomfortable conversation, but I promised Mr. Arnold I would talk to you. Because I do understand. And I'm on your side. But there are some things you could do to help yourself. To, well, not stand out so much. Like, for example . . . what's your real name?"

"KT," KT said.

"No, I mean your full name. What's 'KT' stand for?"

"Kaitlin," KT said. "Kaitlin Therese."

She had actually gone by "Katie" up until fifth grade. Then one Sunday night, coming back from a softball tournament five hours away, she'd been sitting in the back of the family SUV with the entire weekend's worth of homework spread across her lap. (As she remembered it, the teachers in fifth grade always acted like homework was Very Important. And they gave a lot.) It had occurred to her that she could get everything done that much faster if she eliminated the three unnecessary letters from her name.

The other girls on her team had been so impressed with

her stroke of genius—and jealous that KT was the only one who could pare her name down so easily.

Besides, "KT" looked more like a softball player's name than "Katie."

"Kaitlin Therese," Mr. Huck said speculatively. He smiled. "See? There you go. Just start telling people to call you Kaitlin Therese. They'll start thinking of you differently. They'll—"

"You want me to change who I am?" KT asked. Her voice came out as an indignant squawk. Even if Mr. Huck was crazy, she shouldn't have to put up with this. "Change my whole identity?"

"No, no, not that," Mr. Huck said soothingly. "You'd still be KT underneath. This is just temporary, just to help you get along. Just to survive middle school."

"I am surviving middle school," KT snarled. "I'm surviving it *fine*. Just last night at the Rysdale Invitational—"

She broke off, partly because she didn't know what to say about the Rysdale Invitational. Had her team won or lost?

But, also—Mr. Huck's face stayed so *blank*.

Yeah, he's a lacrosse person, not a softball person, but he knows I was playing a big tournament this weekend, KT thought. *We talked about it in class on Friday.*

Mr. Huck always started his Friday classes by asking if anyone had big plans for the weekend. Last Friday KT had mentioned the Rysdale tournament, and how hard her team had worked just to qualify to play in it. She'd said it was the biggest tournament of the winter season for girls her age any-where in the entire country. Mr. Huck had looked right at her the whole time she was talking. He'd asked questions. He'd seemed impressed. It wasn't like when Kona Briggs talked about her piano recital and Mr. Huck half listened while taking attendance or checking his e-mail. And when KT had finished talking, Mr. Huck had said, "Well, class, don't you think we should congratulate KT—and wish her team luck—by giving her a round of applause?"

It had been a nice moment. One of the best things that had ever happened to KT in a social-studies class.

How could Mr. Huck have forgotten all of that now?

Somehow KT was afraid to ask.

"I'm going to class," she said, pulling her arm back and whirling away from him.

She'd barely gone two steps before Mr. Huck said in an embarrassed way, "Uh, KT? This way."

She turned around and saw that he was holding open the door of the nearest classroom.

She looked at the door, looked at the hallway beyond them—*yeah, that is Mr. Huck's room. But have there always been archways and another hall across from it? Why did I get so confused before?*

She stepped into the classroom and headed toward the back. All year long she'd sat beneath a poster that said GEOGRAPHY: IT'S WHERE YOU'RE AT!

But the poster wasn't there anymore.

Neither was her desk, or any other.

Instead the entire room was filled with treadmills.

Chapter *five*

Keep your head down and pitch.

That was the Coach Mike advice that ran through KT's mind now. It dated back to a game KT's team had played during a violent windstorm last summer. Rain never fell, and the lightning sirens never went off, so the two teams kept playing and playing and playing, even though some of the girls were struggling just to stay upright in the extreme gusts. Later one of the team dads found a news story online saying that the winds in the area had actually measured at tornado-force speeds, so at the end-of-season party there'd been huge signs posted: *Our Girls Can Outplay a Tornado—What's Next? A Hurricane?* And *Our Girls 14; Tornado 0.*

Now the words "Keep your head down and pitch" propelled KT to step onto the only empty treadmill in the classroom. It was situated roughly in the same area of the room where her desk had been on Friday. She glanced around and saw that everyone else in the class seemed to be running at the exact same pace. She set her treadmill to level 5, the same numeral glowing on the panel of the treadmill beside hers.

"Not going for ten today?" the boy beside her—Sammy something—muttered. "Not gonna act like you're twice as good as everyone else?"

"Uh, no," KT said uncertainly.

Why did he sound so hostile? What had KT ever done to him? Sammy had sat on the other side of the room until last week. She didn't even know him. He didn't know her.

Keep your head down and pitch, KT told herself. *Keep your head down and pitch.*

Or, in this case, run.

KT's treadmill jerked to life slowly at first and then . . . well, it stayed slow. Level five was barely more than a stroll. For KT's long legs it was an uncomfortable speed, just a tad too fast to walk, but not quite fast enough to run. Without thinking, she punched the speed control up to six, then seven. Then eight.

"So, not twice as good, just sixty percent better?" Sammy sneered beside her.

Was he still talking about her treadmill speed? Why would he care?

"This is going to be great conditioning for softball," KT said, trying to sound a little apologetic even though she didn't know what she had to apologize for. "Did . . . did the school start some new fitness program? Is that what's going on today?"

Maybe there'd been some announcement last Friday about today being Fitness Day. As well as Dress Like a Nerd Day. Last Friday KT had been so focused on thinking about the Rysdale Invitational, she could have missed any number of announcements.

Sammy just gave her a weird look and punched up the speed controls on his own treadmill. Level six, seven, eight, nine . . . Sammy was a lot shorter and stockier than KT, and nine was too fast for him. He was huffing and puffing inside of a minute.

"Samuel," Mr. Huck said from the front of the room. "Remember to think about stamina. Are you going to be able to maintain that speed all period long?"

"KT sped up too," Sammy said.

"You worry about your own speed," Mr. Huck said. He walked back to Sammy's treadmill and punched it back to five. "Let KT worry about KT."

He left KT alone.

But "Let KT worry about KT" threatened to crowd out "Keep your head down and pitch" as the words that played themselves again and again in KT's mind, flowing to the rhythm of her feet pounding on the treadmill.

KT was worried.

There's got to be a logical explanation for everything, KT told herself. *Like, I just didn't hear the announcement about Fitness Day. And Sammy's just a jerk. And so was Maria in homeroom. And Mrs. Whitbourne. Anyhow, at least I must have convinced Mr. Huck not to call me Kaitlin Therese.*

KT set a new goal for herself. She would get through the rest of her morning classes however she could. Then at lunch she'd figure everything out. She always sat with her friends Molly and Lex, and Lex had an iPhone. She'd let KT borrow it, and KT could look up the results to the Rysdale Invitational. That was really all that mattered. Everything else would fall into place once she knew if her team had won or lost.

Just to make sure she didn't get lost again, KT followed kids from her first-period class who were also in her second-period class, kids from her second-period class who were also in her third-period class, and kids from her third-period class who were also in fourth period.

KT didn't talk to any of them, even though some of them were friends. KT didn't trust herself to sound or act normal, not when things were so strange.

But why aren't any of them talking to me? KT wondered. Then she made herself stop wondering, reminding herself, *Keep your head down and pitch. Keep your head down and pitch. Just make it to lunch and everything will be okay.*

In second period, which was supposed to be math, the desks were all replaced with exercise bikes.

During third period, which was usually English, they did stretches again. KT guessed it was supposed to be something like yoga.

Fourth period would have been KT's favorite on a normal day, since she walked in to find bushel baskets full of balls on one side of the room and targets painted on the opposite wall. Clearly, science class had been turned into pitching practice.

But the questions she'd been trying to ignore broke past her careful resolve in fourth period.

Why isn't anyone else saying anything like, "Wow, this is a lot better than science"? Why aren't the brainiacs moaning, "We're not going to get a grade on this, are we?"

KT stepped up to take her first pitch. Bull's-eye! She hit the target dead-on. A red digital number lit up above the target: 52 MPH.

Oh, sweet! KT thought. *They've got a monitor set up*

measuring our pitching speed. I know I can do better than fifty-two.

She grabbed her next ball and hurled it. The number went up: fifty-nine, which was good even for KT.

She reached for a third ball—and felt a hand on her arm stopping her.

"KT, you've got to give someone else a turn," the teacher, Mrs. Sanchez, said.

"That's okay. She can pitch for me," the kid behind her said.

"I've got a better idea—why doesn't she pitch for all of us?" someone else suggested. KT saw it was Rob Mozier, who was kind of the class clown.

KT expected Mrs. Sanchez to laugh, because Rob could make anything sound funny. But Mrs. Sanchez just fixed him with a stern gaze.

"Because you all need to know how to pitch," Mrs. Sanchez said, pulling KT back. "Sorry, KT."

"That's okay. I guess there wasn't money enough to bring in thirty targets and monitors so everyone in the class could use them all at once, not when . . ." KT was ready to say, *not when we're just doing one day of fitness training.* But that made her think, *How was there money to bring in even ten targets and monitors for one day of fitness training? And all those treadmills and exercise bikes and floor mats . . .*

"It's true, there's never enough money in education," Mrs. Sanchez said with a sad shrug.

Exactly, KT thought. *So why would they put on such an elaborate fitness day?*

Maybe they'd gotten some grant, something related to

childhood obesity or something like that. But one day of exercising wasn't going to make any difference. And if they wanted to get kids interested in exercising, why weren't they playing games and having fun with it, instead of just doing drills and practice?

Don't worry about it, KT told herself. *Just get through this class and get to lunch.*

Even when she broke into the sixties on her next turn to pitch, she couldn't quite enjoy it.

The bell rang at the end of fourth period, sending everyone to lunch. KT was very careful to follow the crowd, just in case the cafeteria had become as difficult to find as the library. And that bothered her—she wasn't a follower. She was a leader. She was a star pitcher, after all.

Just find Molly and Lex, she told herself. *Just borrow Lex's iPhone and find out who won the Rysdale Invitational. Then they can help you make sense of everything else.*

The other two girls weren't waiting for KT at the end of the food line, so KT guessed that they'd packed their lunches.

Nothing unusual about that, KT told herself.

But she had nervous tremors in her stomach as she loaded up her own tray with food: two slices of pizza, a salad, a bowlful of grapes.

You're just hungry, KT told herself. *You burned off a lot of calories this morning.*

She tapped in her student ID number at the checkout and turned to face the cafeteria.

Molly and Lex were sitting in their usual spot in the center of the room, with an empty spot on the bench across from them.

They saved me a seat, KT thought, relief flowing over her.

Though there was no reason to feel surprised. Her friends always saved her a seat.

KT rushed over to them and slid her tray onto the table. Even as she dropped into the chair, she held out her hand.

"Hey, Lex, give me your phone and I'll show you some amazing video from last night," KT said. This was a gamble, but only a small one. Parents were always videotaping parts of her team's games, and odds were somebody had already posted something online. She could search for some video right after she looked at the Rysdale website.

KT reached across the table toward Lex's sweatshirt pocket, where she always kept her phone.

Lex jerked away and put her hand over her pocket, protecting the phone from KT.

"No, thanks," she said in a stiff, artificial voice. "I don't feel like watching anything right now."

The way Lex was staring at KT, it was like KT had grabbed Lex's sandwich and tried to take a big bite out of it.

No, scratch that. KT and Molly and Lex ate one another's food all the time. This was more like a total *stranger* had come up to Lex and taken a bite out of her sandwich.

Or—someone she didn't like.

"No, really. You'll love this video," KT persisted. But a strange tone had entered her voice.

KT sounded like she was begging.

And she'd pulled back her hand, like she didn't really expect Lex to hand over the phone.

"KT," Molly said, and her voice was just as stiff and fake as Lex's had been. "We're kind of busy right now. We're talking about math."

Somehow, the way she said "math" was like putting up a fence—a fence that shut out KT.

KT remembered that, in addition to playing on the school softball team, Molly and Lex were in some after-school math club, and took extra tests four or five times a year. KT figured their parents probably made them do that—who would take extra math tests if they didn't have to?

"Oh, *math*," KT said scornfully. "Well, we all know what's really important, don't we?"

This was supposed to be a cue for Molly and Lex to put their heads together and sing out, "Softball!" And then one of them would ask about the Rysdale Invitational, and they'd talk about their own club teams and the school softball season and . . .

Molly just looked at KT.

"Uh, right," Molly said. Now she glanced over at Lex, and there was definitely an eye roll involved.

"*You* know," KT said, and now she sounded truly desperate, as bad as a batter reaching back for a fastball that had already crossed the plate.

But Molly and Lex weren't even listening. They were staring past KT now, toward the crowd of kids still coming out of the lunch line.

"Evangeline!" they cried, in unison. Their faces glowed with practically identical mixes of delight and awe.

That's how they usually greet me, KT thought, feeling an unusual stab of jealousy.

She turned around and it was just weird old Evangeline Rangel behind her. Everybody said Evangeline was the smartest kid in school. She'd skipped a grade back in elementary school—maybe even two. Even now, though she was tech-nically still a seventh grader, she took most of her classes with the eighth grade or even over at the high school. Rumors occasionally flew about Evangeline: She'd written a thousand-page novel that was going to be published. . . . She'd gotten invited to go to some special school where everyone was a genius. . . . Mr. Shiwawa had admitted in front of the whole class that Evangeline knew more about science than he did, so she didn't have to do any homework at all, just work on some special project that would probably go straight to the CIA when it was finished, it'd be that important. . . .

But most of the talk about Evangeline was about how strange she was. Supposedly she still played with dolls. She'd told somebody her dearest dream was to write Greek with one hand and Latin with the other, like President Garfield had been able to do back in the 1800s. (Who else even knew there'd been a President Garfield?) She'd stare off into space in class, and then when the teacher called on her, she'd say something like, "I was trying to tell if I could feel the gap between air molecules . . ." Because of skipping all those grades, she was smaller than the other kids, and her mother still dressed her in little-girl dresses. She wore her hair like a little girl too, with pigtails dangling from high up on either side of her head, instead of one normal ponytail in the back.

KT tried to think if she had ever seen Evangeline in the cafeteria before—maybe back in the corner, alone, hunched over a book.

"Here, Evangeline," Molly said eagerly, moving her brown paper sack to make room. "Sit down."

"KT, do you *mind*?" Lex said.

KT jerked back, slow to understand. *Did they mean—? Could it be—?*

She slid over, cramming herself into a space that really wasn't big enough.

"Thanks," Lex muttered as Evangeline sat down, but it sounded more like she meant, *What took you so long?*

"Let me guess—you're talking about math, right?" Evangeline said, grinning, as she turned her back on KT. The pigtail on the right side of Evangeline's head slapped KT in the face.

And KT, totally blocked off from her friends, finally got it.

Molly and Lex hadn't been saving a seat for her.

They'd been saving it for Evangeline.

Chapter Six

It's April Fools' Day, KT thought, even though she knew it wasn't. It was only early February.

It's Backward Day, as well as Dress Like a Nerd Day and Fitness Day, KT thought. *This is some wacky role-playing thing the guidance department set up, where you're supposed to be nice to people you're usually mean to, and vice versa, and Molly and Lex are actually going along with it. They'll laugh about it with me after school.*

By sixth period this was the best explanation KT could come up with.

Sixth period had been transformed from Spanish class into weight-training class.

KT pumped iron listlessly, trying not to think about how crazy it was that the school had brought in thirty weight machines just for one day of use.

Seventh period was supposed to be phys ed class, and KT wondered what *that* would turn out to be. But as she walked through the hall, trying to find someone to follow to class, she heard an announcement over the PA system: "All students report to the end-of-school pep rally at this time. Repeat, report to the pep rally."

All right! KT thought.

The school pep rallies were always kind of cheesy, but KT loved them anyway. Brecksville North had three over the course of the year: one for the fall sports, one for the winter sports, and one for the spring sports. This had to be the one kicking off the start of the school's spring sports season.

Softball, baseball, lacrosse, track . . . , KT thought, listing all the sports. In order of importance, of course.

KT still remembered how she'd felt last year, standing on the floor of the gym with her softball teammates while the whole school cheered around them. It had felt like everybody loved her, like they wanted her to win as much as she did.

The principal had talked about how she and the other athletes were the "best of the best."

"We are so proud to have them representing our school," he'd said. "They will be carrying Brecksville North pride and honor onto the playing field with them."

It wasn't just team spirit or school spirit that KT had felt pulsing through the gym that day. It was more like patriotism—like KT and her fellow athletes were warriors, being sent out to win some righteous war.

Of course, KT couldn't say something like that out loud, not even to Molly and Lex. But she'd seen the pride glowing on their faces too. They had to have felt the same way.

Now she saw Molly's blond head and Lex's dark one bobbing in the crowd ahead of her.

"Molly, Lex—wait up!" she called, because surely whatever silly role-play they'd been doing at lunch would be over by now. Surely they'd want to walk into the gym with her.

But Molly and Lex didn't seem to hear. The crowd cut them off. KT tried to shove her way forward. Strangely, nobody was letting her past.

"*Excuse* me," KT said, barreling forward anyhow.

She rammed into what seemed to be a wall. No, it was a person—Mr. Horace, the meanest math teacher in the whole school. KT felt very lucky that she'd always managed to avoid getting him. But physically he wasn't very imposing: He was a frail, white-haired old man. The joke going around school was that some kids had supposedly seen him moussing his hair to look like Albert Einstein's.

KT was just glad she hadn't actually knocked him down.

"Oh, sorry, Mr. Horace," she apologized. "I was trying to catch up with my team."

She started to step around him, but Mr. Horace lashed out his hand and grabbed her arm. He had a surprisingly strong grip for such an old man.

"You!" he cried. "You are KT Sutton, correct?"

"Uh, yes," KT said. "Yes, sir."

Mr. Horace's eyes narrowed into slits.

"*You* don't have a team," he snarled.

KT felt her own eyes go wide with surprise. Why was Mr. Horace giving her a hard time? She wouldn't have even said he knew who she was. Was this his idea of a joke? Sometimes teachers did have strange senses of humor.

"Yes, I do," KT corrected him. "I'm on the softball team. I'm the pitcher. Believe me, they need me this year!"

She grinned, in case Mr. Horace was joking and she needed to joke back.

She tried to pull her arm back and get away from Mr. Horace. But he tightened his grip and pulled her to the side.

"Let me tell you something, young lady," he said, leaning close and practically spitting in her face. "I do not appreciate your disrespect. It's unconscionable. I don't know what you were planning, but this year's teams are the most dedicated, hardest-working students I've ever seen, and I will *not* have them denied the honor they deserve."

"Mr. Horace, I don't know what you're talking about," KT protested. "I'm not planning anything!"

She glanced around, hoping Molly and Lex were still nearby and would come to her defense. Wasn't that what teammates were for? They were in math club—maybe Mr. Horace actually liked them.

It didn't matter. They'd already disappeared through the next doorway.

The kids around her in the hall were doing that classic middle-school thing of staring while pretending to be walking nonchalantly by.

"Don't know what I'm talking about!" Mr. Horace huffed. "Then I'll spell it out. You, young lady, are not on any team. And yet you're trying to walk through that door"—he pointed toward the entryway ahead of them—"which is *only* for team members. You do *not* belong here. I would venture to say that you do not even belong at this school, with the attitude you've displayed! I—"

"Mr. Horace, I'll make sure she goes in the right door," a voice interrupted from behind KT.

KT turned and saw Mr. Huck. He grabbed her other arm and tugged her in the opposite direction.

For a moment it seemed like Mr. Horace was going to keep arguing—and keep pulling on KT's arm, like he and Mr. Huck were playing some bizarre game of tug-of-war.

But then he abruptly let go, sending KT reeling sideways. KT knocked into Mr. Huck, and Mr. Huck clutched her arm tighter. Now it felt like he was trying to hold her up.

"Be sure that you do," Mr. Horace growled at Mr. Huck. "I won't have her ruining this pep rally!"

Then Mr. Horace turned on his heel and sped through the next doorway.

A split second later a swelling chorus of "Yay! Hurray! Go team!" rolled out from the direction of the doorway, almost as if the pep rally crowd was cheering Mr. Horace.

But of course that was ridiculous. Everybody hated him.

"You do *not* mess with Mr. Horace on a game day," Mr. Huck snapped at KT.

"Game day?" KT repeated, still baffled. She jerked her arm away from Mr. Huck. "He's just a math teacher!"

Mr. Huck seemed to be studying her face closely. He shook his head.

"I understand how you feel," he said. "But think this through. You are not helping your cause. You're making it harder and harder for me to defend you."

"Defend me? From what? And—what cause?" KT asked. She stood up perfectly straight, and the motion reminded her of the moment before every pitch when she drew herself to her full height. This steadied her, let her focus on what she really needed to say. "I'm the best pitcher in the eighth grade. I *deserve* this pep rally!"

Mr. Huck stopped shaking his head and winced.

"I agree with you," he said. "I totally agree with you. But this is not the way to get what you want. You're dancing dangerously close to insubordination. Look. Go sit in the stands with the other students. Put your hands over your ears if you have to. But don't do anything that's going to have Mr. Horace begging for your suspension or expulsion. Don't do anything that'll go on your permanent record. Colleges don't usually look at middle-school behavior, but for the kind of scholarships you're going to be up for . . ."

Permanent record? KT thought. *Suspension? Expulsion? Insubordination?*

Mr. Huck could not be talking about anything connected to a pep rally. He could not be talking about anything that had any link to KT.

On a normal day KT would have laughed it off. She would have pulled away from Mr. Huck and walked right through the doorway behind Mr. Horace and Molly and Lex.

But today had been too strange. KT needed something like a time-out in softball—a step away from the pitching circle just long enough to get her thoughts together. To refocus and decide what to do.

"Mr. Huck, I think . . . I think I need to go to the bathroom," KT said.

Mr. Huck looked relieved.

"Under the circumstances, that's probably a great idea," he said. He pointed back toward the girls' room KT had already passed on her way down the hall. "Go on. Hide out for the entire pep rally, if you want. I won't tell anyone."

He knows I don't really need to go to the bathroom, KT thought. *But . . . why does he think I need to hide?*

KT stumbled backward, almost tripping in her eagerness to get away. She scurried into the bathroom. She splashed water on her face and stood there, leaning on the sink. In the mirror, her face was still flushed, angry spots of color showing high on each cheek. Her dark eyes were wide and dazed.

"I do deserve this pep rally," she whispered to her own image. "Go take what you deserve! Go for it!"

But she couldn't quite bring herself to stomp out of the bathroom and on into the gym.

The noise of the other kids pounding down the hall ceased. Dimly, KT could hear the boom of the PA system from the pep rally—no actual words, just the pounding bass and then the roar of the crowd.

When it's time to introduce the softball team, everyone will notice I'm not there, KT told herself. *Any minute now someone will be yelling into the bathroom, "Come on, KT! We can't do this without you!"*

KT waited, enjoying this image, enjoying the thought of seeing Mr. Huck's and Mr. Horace's faces when they saw how wrong they'd been about everything.

Nobody came for KT.

This is my last pep rally of middle school, she thought. *And I'm missing it.*

KT heard pounding feet in the hallway again, the revved-up sound of kids fleeing school.

Correction, she thought. *I missed it.*

She drew in a ragged breath.

I need . . . I need . . . softball, she thought.

Fortunately, practice would be right after school. Right now.

Chapter SeV3n

KT had forgotten her glove, her bat, and her cleats when she'd forgotten her phone, iPod, and backpack.

I'll borrow somebody else's phone and call Mom to bring my stuff, KT thought. *Just . . . maybe not Lex's.*

KT went out the door at the side of the school, the one that everyone called the athletic entrance. Usually all the softball girls congregated here, then they walked out to the field behind the school together. Because KT hadn't made a stop in the locker room to get changed, she was the first one out. She leaned her head back against the brick wall and took huge gulps of the fresh, cool air. It tasted like a new season, new possibilities.

I will be the first pitcher in Brecksville North softball history to throw a no-hitter every game, KT thought. *I will.*

That was what she needed to focus on right now. Not the oddity of not knowing what had happened at the end of the Rysdale Invitational last night. Not all the strange moments of the school day. Not even the bizarre things Mr. Huck and Mr. Horace had said.

But I will tell Coach Marina how Mr. Horace wouldn't let me go in the right door for the pep rally, KT thought.

She pictured how furious the whole team would be on her behalf. Scarlet, who was a bit of a drama queen, would probably hug her and say, *We were so worried about you when you didn't show up!* Nevia, who was always outraged when things weren't fair, would say, *Mr. Horace owes you a letter of apology. No—he owes you a whole new pep rally! One just for you!*

Maybe there would be a pep rally just for KT—or, anyhow, a recognition ceremony in front of the whole school—if KT did manage to have a season full of no-hitters and the school retired her jersey in her honor. Probably they'd do that at eighth-grade graduation. Everybody's parents would be there for that too. She pictured the SUTTON 32 jersey hanging in the school trophy case alongside Will Stern's, Haley Blake's, and Roger Gonzalez's, there for everyone to see, every time anyone entered the building, for years to come.

Then she remembered the jerseys had been missing that morning. Replaced by desks, of all things.

Out here in the fresh air, moments away from softball practice, it was easy to dismiss that.

It was probably just some prank, KT thought. *Probably it's some huge scandal and someone got in awful trouble. I just didn't hear about it because I was so distracted all day long, worrying about the Rysdale Invitational.*

KT drew more fresh air into her lungs, and another idea occurred to her.

Or maybe it was connected to the pep rally and Fitness

Day, she thought. *Maybe it was like a test, to see how many students notice the jerseys were missing. To make sure everyone appreciates the school's history.*

She could easily imagine Mr. Arnold bringing that up at the pep rally. He would have rolled out the phrase "this school's rich athletic heritage" or something like that. He would have made sure every kid at the pep rally remembered the names Will Stern, Haley Blake, and Roger Gonzalez.

And next year my name will be on that list too, KT told herself.

Or it would be if the rest of the team ever showed up.

Since she didn't have her phone, KT couldn't check the time. But it seemed like at least ten or fifteen minutes had passed since the end of school. Coach Marina was a stickler about people showing up promptly. Where was everyone?

KT looked around for someone to ask about the time. The area around the athletic entrance was usually packed this time of day, not just with softball players, but with kids from all the other sports too. It was funny how they all had their own section of wall that they leaned against: The softball girls always stood between the baseball team and the lacrosse guys.

But today KT was the only one standing at the athletic entrance.

Maybe . . . maybe I was really late, not really early? she thought. *Maybe everyone else is already out on the field?*

She didn't see how that could be possible, but she launched herself away from the wall and raced around behind the school, toward the softball diamond.

As soon as she turned the corner of the building, KT realized she was following a perfect angle: She was running toward the same view she'd seen dozens of times during practices and games as she raced to get to first base. There was the tacky mauve house with all the concrete geese out front, the one that KT always hoped would distract visiting teams. There was the row of white and cream-colored and tan houses beside it, the ones so bland and boringly decorated that KT hoped the sight of them would put visiting teams to sleep.

KT turned her head and dropped her gaze, to line up her view with home base.

It wasn't there.

In fact—now that KT looked more closely—none of the bases were there.

Neither was the pitching circle.

Neither was the backstop.

Neither were the benches.

Neither were the bleachers.

KT stopped running.

She glanced around frantically, hoping she'd just become disoriented again and the softball field—with the full softball team on it—would be just a little bit to the right or a little bit to the left, just slightly out of her line of vision.

But it wasn't.

The baseball field was supposed to be a little bit to the right, and it wasn't there either. The track/football stadium was supposed to be a little bit to the left, and it had vanished too.

So had the lacrosse fields.

So had the soccer fields.

So had the tennis courts.

The vast sports complex that lay behind Brecksville Middle School North had been turned into nothing but a wide open field of grass.

Chapter Eight

"No," KT whispered.

This was the first odd thing that had happened all day that she could find no explanation for, even a lame one.

But she still tried. All she had to do was focus on what really mattered.

Maybe . . . maybe . . . the softball field is temporarily gone, for whatever reason, but of course there's still softball practice, she told herself. *There's still a softball team. Maybe they're just practicing in the gym today.*

They did that sometimes, especially early in the season. Usually that was only when it was rainy or bitterly cold, and today was both sunny and just slightly, pleasingly cool. But KT turned eagerly and started heading back toward the gym.

It wasn't there either.

The huge dome at the back of the building that arced over the gym had been flattened, as if ironed out by a giant. And there were *windows* all along the section of wall that should have been an unbroken stretch of brick.

Windows like that would never last in a gym.

KT stared, trying to get her eyes to see the school building right. Softball was a fairly portable sport—bases, baselines, and even benches and backstops and bleachers could be moved without too much trouble. The same was true of baseball, lacrosse, and soccer. (Her mind skipped over the more elaborate setups of tennis and the track/football stadium.) But the gym—the gym was the heart of the school. The whole building would have to be redone to eliminate the gym from Brecksville Middle School North.

It was, KT told herself. *That's why the rooflines looked off when I got close to the front of the school this morning. That's why I got lost looking for the library. That's why so many of my classes were in the wrong places.*

But how could that have happened over a single weekend? How could that explain why every class had been turned into a fitness fest? Or why Molly and Lex had saved a seat for Evangeline instead of KT at lunch? Or why everyone, the entire day long, had said such strange things and acted so mean to KT?

Or why KT still couldn't remember what had happened at the end of the Rysdale championship game?

KT whirled around and took off running. For the first few steps she wasn't sure what she was running toward, but her feet seemed to know.

Home, she realized. *I'm going home.*

The rest of her plan kicked in even as she ran. The image she held in her mind—the image pulling her home—was the trophy shrine in the family room. All she had to do was see it, with all the trophies back in their proper places, dust-free, and the Rysdale trophy right in the center. As soon as she saw the Rysdale trophy—and picked it up and held it and read off the words CHAMPION or FIRST RUNNER-UP—then she was sure everything else would make sense.

Even the missing gym.

Even the missing softball diamond.

Even Mr. Huck's and Mr. Horace's crazy babblings.

Even Molly and Lex giving KT's saved seat to Evangeline at lunch.

KT ran faster.

By the time she turned onto her own street, she was racing flat-out, like someone fleeing desperately toward home plate ahead of the catcher.

She hit the front door—*oops, don't have my key*—and dashed around to the garage door instead. She stabbed her fingers against the garage door control pad (secret code 2024, the year she hoped to play in the Olympics, or at least the softball World Cup). The door lurched open, but she was too impatient to wait. She bent down and commando-crawled under it as soon as there was the slightest gap.

Both her parents' cars were gone, so she sprinted easily across the garage floor, covering the entire distance in four steps. She slammed through the next door into the house, dashed through the kitchen, and raced into the family room. The afternoon sunshine was streaming down onto the shrine, creating a dazzling gleam of golden glory.

KT let out a sigh, because somehow, though she hadn't quite let herself think it, she'd been a little bit afraid that the trophies would still be missing, that they would have disappeared as completely as the gym and the softball diamond.

"Proof," KT said aloud.

She wiped sweat off her forehead and tiptoed reverently toward the shrine, even as she admired the glow of the sunlight on gold.

KT had played in a different tournament practically every weekend the past few years, except for during the school softball season last spring. (That had been games twice a week, and only two weekend tournaments. A vacation of sorts, which had left KT feeling antsy and longing to get back to serious ball.) Not every single tournament she'd played in had given trophies to the individual players, but a lot of them had, particularly when she was younger. She had trophies in the shrine dating back to her first season of T-ball, way back in kindergarten. And she had a few random trophies from other sports—soccer, basketball, lacrosse—from when she was too young to be on teams offering year-round softball. But mostly the shrine looked like an entire softball team's worth of golden running girls atop their trophies, with enough golden gloves, bats, and balls on neighboring trophies to fully equip them.

So why couldn't KT lay her gaze on a single running girl, glove, bat, or ball trophy right at the moment?

She picked up the nearest trophy, the one in the spot she had assumed would belong to the Rysdale Invitational prize. This trophy had a rectangular gold chunk atop a slender pedestal. The rectangle had a fake-looking keypad of numbers.

Is that supposed to be a calculator? KT wondered. *Why? Is it supposed to be something about calculating our chances of*

*winning nationals, too, or of calculating our massive college
scholarships, or . . .*

KT gave up on trying to figure out this craziness and
glanced down at the metal plaque at the base of the trophy.

FIRST PLACE, it said.

"Yes! Yes! Yes!" KT cried, holding the trophy aloft and
pumping her arm up and down with every "yes!"

She looked back at the plaque, wanting to see those lovely,
golden letters: RYSDALE INVITATIONAL underneath the FIRST
PLACE.

That wasn't what it said.

Instead the words were BLAIRTON MATH COMPETITION.

Math? KT thought. *Math?*

She slammed the trophy back onto the shelf, pounding it
down so hard that the whole shelf shook. She grabbed the
next trophy over, which was topped with another golden calculator. The plaque on this one read FIRST PLACE, FEASEL MATH
INVITATIONAL, MAXWELL CHARLES SUTTON.

Max? KT thought. *Max has math trophies? How could that
be?*

She began pulling trophies off the shelf at random. They
were topped with more calculators, with pencils, with desks,
with bronzed versions of the symbol for pi. She dropped them
and kept grabbing the next trophies back.

*Calculator, calculator, pencil. Calculator, desk, piece of
paper . . .*

Every single one of them was Max's.

What had happened to all of KT's trophies?

Chapter Nine

"Kaitlin Therese!"

KT was still frantically pulling trophies off the shelf when she heard her mother scream behind her. She'd apparently just gotten home—KT could hear the garage door jerking shut behind her.

"Just *what* do you think you're *doing*?" Mom shrieked, in a tone KT had never heard her use before.

"My trophies—where are my trophies?" KT wailed. "Why did you have to replace them all with Max's?"

"Oh, for crying out loud," Mom said. She crossed the family room in three angry strides, and dived toward the lowest, most out-of-the-way shelf. "They're right here, right where they've always been."

She held up a three-inch-tall figure on a wooden base—not really big enough for KT to consider it a trophy. But she squinted at the cheap-looking plaque at the bottom:

KT SUTTON

SEVENTH-GRADE

HONOR ROLL

"Here's the other one," Mom said, holding up a twin of the first, except that this one said SIXTH-GRADE HONOR ROLL. "Before that, back in elementary school, they just gave out certificates. They're here too."

She rifled through a stack of papers.

"That's not what I meant!" KT protested.

The anger in Mom's face softened slightly.

"KT, you know your father and I are very proud of you *and* Max," she said. "It's just, you have different talents, and your particular talents don't happen to lead to lots and lots of trophies. But—"

"Yes, they do!" KT shrieked. "Where did you put them? Why did you take all mine away and bring in these, these *bogus* trophies for Max?"

He'd never been on any math team. Not that KT knew of, anyway, and wouldn't she know something like that if he'd won all these trophies? The only trophy Max should have in the shrine was his one PARTICIPATION trophy from kindergarten, the one year he did T-ball before quitting sports altogether.

She swung her hand at a row of calculator- and pencil-topped trophies, toppling them like so many bowling pins.

"He doesn't deserve any of this!" KT screamed.

All the sympathy and concern in Mom's expression vanished. Her face hardened into a mask of fury.

"That," she snarled, "was completely uncalled for. I don't know what you're talking about. You know how hard Max works! You do not build yourself up by tearing down your brother! I won't allow it!"

She grabbed KT by the shoulders and gave her a rough shake.

"But—," KT protested.

"You have five minutes," Mom said, shoving KT away. "Put every single one of these trophies back where they belong. Then get changed. We will be walking out that door to go watch Max at precisely four thirty."

"Watch Max?" KT wailed. "What? Mom, no. I've got to get back to practice."

She said this even though she didn't know where practice was, even though the gym and the softball field had vanished. It was something to hold on to, something to wish for.

She longed for softball practice.

Even as KT spoke, Mom had started to stomp away. But now she whirled back around and glared.

"And now you're lying to me?" Mom asked incredulously. "KT, I *know* your schedule. It's easy to keep track of. You don't have anything after school today! Not anything that *you're* doing!"

"Then I must have . . . homework," KT said, even though she couldn't quite remember if she did or not.

Mom went back to angrily stomping away.

"I can't even look at you right now," she called over her shoulder. "Do what I told you!"

KT gazed down at the toppled trophies before her, and at the half dozen she'd left standing. She swung both arms out, knocking down every single one.

Chapter ten

It was a tense ride in the car.

Dad drummed his fingers on the steering wheel. Mom squeezed her hands together so hard her knuckles turned white.

"Max'll do fine," Dad said.

In the backseat KT seethed.

Why are they making me go watch some stupid thing with Max? KT wondered. *Why aren't they insisting I get back to practice?*

Her parents were fanatical about the importance of practice. They routinely left work early to get her to her club-team practices. Dad had even driven her there once when he'd had a 103-degree fever and had to stop twice by the side of the road to lean his head out the door to vomit.

But KT couldn't say anything else about softball practice.

She couldn't, because all of her sports trophies had vanished.

She couldn't, because when she'd gone up to her room, she'd looked for her list of goals on her bulletin board—about pitching for the University of Arizona, about winning a gold medal in the Olympics—and it had vanished too.

In its place had been a row of report cards.

All with straight As.

Her pictures of the 2004 and 2008 Olympic softball teams were missing as well, along with the hand-lettered sign that said, *IT'S COMING BACK! IT HAS TO! AND I'LL PLAY IN THE OLYMPICS IN 2024!*

She'd quickly logged on to her laptop—no messing around with the iPod this time—and still couldn't find the Rysdale Invitational website.

She couldn't find the "Bring softball back to the Olympics!" Facebook page.

She couldn't find the Amateur Softball Association website.

At that point Dad had barged into her room—just home from work, judging from his suit and tie—and said, "I don't want to hear a single word about the argument you tried to start with your mother. Or anything else. You are not going to ruin this day for your mother or Max or me. You are getting in the car, and you are getting in that car *now*!"

KT got.

Mom and Dad are acting strange, but they're not acting like they think there's anything strange going on, KT thought. *They're acting like they think everything is normal.*

She thought of Mom holding up that stupid honor-roll trophy and saying, "They're right here, right where they've always been."

Like that was all KT had ever earned.

How could Mom have forgotten all of KT's softball trophies? How could Mom have forgotten KT's softball practice?

How could the softball field and the gym have disappeared? How could the entire softball team—and the coach— have failed to show up for practice? How could Mr. Horace have told me I wasn't on a team? How could this whole day have been so mixed-up and confusing?

Dad turned onto the street in front of the school.

"The lot by the academic entrance already looks full," he said. "You want to try out front?"

"Sure," Mom said.

Academic entrance? KT thought scornfully.

But the front parking lot was full too. Dad ended up having to park three blocks away.

Mom spun around in her seat, glancing at KT for the first time since she'd slid into the car.

"You didn't change?" she cried in dismay.

KT looked down at her clothes, which were admittedly a little sweaty after her day of jogging, pitching, exercise-biking, and weight training. And after running to and from school.

"I like these clothes," KT said.

"But—," Mom began.

Dad put his hand warningly on Mom's arm.

"Brenda," he said. "Don't fight this battle right now. KT's here, she's supporting her brother, she's showing school spirit . . . for now, let's just focus on Max, shall we?"

Since when does Dad use terms like "shall we"? KT wondered.

Maybe it was just the aftereffect of all that running, but she felt chilled suddenly. It was all she could do to stumble out of the car.

Dad slammed the door shut behind her.

"Don't try anything," he warned her through gritted teeth. "Don't upset your mother."

What does he think I'm going to try? KT wondered.

They joined a huge crowd walking into the school, buzzing with excitement. Someone—cheerleaders, probably—had lined the hallways with posters: *GO B-NORTH! BEAT WINCHESTER!* And *EVERYBODY KNOWS WE'RE SMARTER!* And *DO THE MATH! BRECKSVILLE NORTH ALWAYS COMES OUT #1!*

KT had been toying with the notion that any competitive event Max played would have to have something to do with video games. Maybe all those gold lumps on his trophies were actually remote controls, not calculators?

But this was definitely a math event they were walking toward. Someone had written out pi to thirty decimal places in huge numerals down the main hallway. Most of the kids KT saw were wearing shirts with numbers and mathematical symbols all over them. Some of the grown-ups were even wearing math T-shirts or sweatshirts or polos. And— KT noticed for the first time—Dad's tie was covered with mathematical notations. Had he come home from work and changed *into* those clothes?

KT silently trailed Mom and Dad into what should have been the gym. Now it looked more like the library.

A library with rows and rows of tall bleachers over-shadowing the bookshelves.

And, facing the bleachers, ten velvet chairs clustered in two groups.

And, above the chairs, huge screens—gigantic SMART boards, maybe?

"Max is bound to get the most playing time of any of the sixth graders," Dad told Mom quietly as they sat down near the front of the bleachers. "If he doesn't, I think we should complain to the coach."

KT glanced around quickly, hoping nobody would see her going to a math competition or—even worse—sitting with her parents. But it looked like practically every kid in the school was there.

Somehow KT couldn't find the courage to go over and sit with any of her friends.

Not after what had happened with Molly and Lex at lunch.

And not when her friends all seemed to be carefully looking away from her.

KT turned around and faced the velvet chairs and pretended she hadn't seen any of her friends, either.

Another couple came in and sat in front of KT's parents. They looked vaguely familiar.

"Eugenia! Morris!" Mom greeted them, pasting on a too-wide smile. "Look, honey, the Bashkovs are here!"

Oh, yeah, KT thought. *Ben's parents.*

Ben Bashkov had been Max's best friend since kindergarten. He was a scrawny little kid who always asked goofy questions like "What if a ghost and a werewolf got into a fight? Who do you think would win?" And "Which do you think has more bacteria in it? Spit or blood?"

Dad clapped Mr. Bashkov on the shoulder and said, "Who's going to be the high scorer on the team today—your son or ours?"

"It does not matter. They are on the same team," Mr.

Bashkov said in his slightly accented English. KT could never be bothered to remember where the Bashkovs had come from—Russia, maybe?

Dad punched Mr. Bashkov on the arm.

"Yeah, I want my son to be the best too!" he said and laughed.

Geez, Dad, KT thought. *Are you this obnoxious at my softball games too?*

Just thinking the word "softball" made KT's heart ache. She half rose, thinking that at least she could look out a window and see if her team was anywhere in sight. But Mom clamped her hand on KT's leg.

"Sit," she hissed.

"You are still doing so well in all your classes, no?" Mrs. Bashkov asked KT. Her tone reminded KT of something. Oh, yeah: Vanessa's mom trying to talk to Max at softball games. The tone said, *I know you're a pathetic loser, but I'm a nice person, so I will at least pretend to be interested.*

Mom squeezed KT's knee, a clear warning: *Don't you dare say anything to embarrass me!*

"Oh, yes," Mom answered before KT had a chance to. "We don't like to brag, of course, but KT has the highest grade point average in eighth grade."

"No, I don't!" KT started to protest, but just then the Brecksville North math team came jogging into the library. Everyone else in the stands rose in one motion and began to cheer: "Two, four, six, eight, who do we appreciate? Our scholars! Our scholars! Our scholars!"

The sound was deafening.

Mom grabbed KT's arm and yanked her into a standing position too.

"Show some respect!" Mom hissed in KT's ear.

Dazed, KT looked around. The stands were completely packed, everyone screaming at the top of their lungs. Some girls were even shaking pom-poms. Others were shrieking like they'd just glimpsed the hottest guys in the school. It was like this was football or basketball—the school sports everyone cared about the most.

And I have the highest grade point average in my class? KT thought scornfully. *Yeah, right.*

The chills from before came back. KT's ears buzzed; her vision went in and out. For a moment she thought she might faint. But her brain kept churning out thoughts, trying to make sense out of insanity.

It all fit. Suddenly KT saw exactly *what* had happened, even though she was still clueless as to how or why.

Last week people had acted like the football and basketball players were gods.

This week it was the math team.

Yesterday she'd been a talented athlete—the star of her team. Today she still had the talent, but where was her team? Suddenly it seemed like the only thing she'd ever accomplished was good grades.

School turned into sports, KT thought. *And sports turned into school.*

How could she possibly change it back?

Chapter Eleven

KT swayed. Mom yanked on her arm, pulling her down to the bleacher seat once again. Evidently everyone was sitting down.

Mrs. Bashkov peered at KT.

"Oh, I get so nervous at these things too," she said, patting KT's leg. "But—are you sure you're all right? You look like you've seen a ghost!"

"KT's fine," Mom said through gritted teeth. She elbowed KT, a subtle reminder that KT was supposed to be acting fine.

Oh, right, the star of the math team couldn't have a difficult sister, could he? KT thought bitterly.

Her head swam. Mrs. Bashkov's patting continued.

"Have you ever played any acs, KT?" Mrs. Bashkov asked. "Have you ever experienced this for yourself?"

"KT prefers to focus on her studies," Mom said. Her elbow seemed to be on the verge of drilling a hole between KT's ribs.

Mom, could you stop acting like I'm your puppet? I can

speak for myself! I can sit and stand and sit again all on my own! KT thought.

But—could she? Was it possible that in this version of the world, KT was as spineless as a rag doll?

No. I'm still a pitcher, KT thought.

Wasn't she?

"KT is in the sports club," Mom said. "But that just meets, like, once a month, and they sit around answering questions about fitness."

Sports club? Never heard of it, KT thought. *Sounds boring. But—softball, Mom. Say I do softball. Please.*

Mom didn't say that. Instead she frowned.

"We've told KT that she's really going to need to step up her involvement in high school," Mom said.

"Yes," Mrs. Bashkov agreed. "I've heard that, even with top grades and test scores, anyone wanting to get into a really good college has to excel at acs, too. But, oh, it would be so hard to get up to speed, picking up a new ac at the high-school level! My Ben's been on one math team or another ever since first grade!"

She patted KT's leg again, but her tone said, *You really are pitiful, aren't you? I'm glad I don't have a kid like you!*

"It's sports," KT muttered. It was sports that kids had to excel at in high school, along with getting good grades and test scores, in order to get into a good college. Everybody knew that.

But this was backward world. Sports had turned into something called "acs."

Oh—academics, KT figured out.

"Did you say something, dear?" Mrs. Bashkov asked, leaning in close.

But she didn't wait for an answer, because an announcer—or was he an umpire? A referee?—had stepped up to a podium located between the two clusters of velvet chairs. That set off another round of cheering from the crowd, and Mrs. Bashkov lapsed into screaming, "Ben! Ben! Ben! Ben!"

The announcer smiled.

"Enthusiastic crowd," he commented. "You'd think this was the biggest rivalry in the entire league. Oh, that's right—it is!"

The crowd roared again.

"I'll introduce the visiting team first," the announcer said. "Starting for the Winchester Wits, Gertrude Iris Collins, Harvey Frederick Gustafson, Emma Marie Valero . . ."

Five kids jumped up from benches at the back of the room and, pumping their arms, raced toward one cluster of velvet chairs. The girls were wearing matching plaid jumpers and knee-high socks; the boys were in khakis, blue blazers, and plaid ties.

"Nerd city," KT muttered to herself. Even a math team should be able to come up with better uniforms. Something that looked more . . . athletic, maybe?

But behind her she could hear girls crying out, "Oh, he's hot!" and "I'd so go out with him!"

As soon as the Winchester team sat down, a crew of helpers carried out five desks and positioned them in front of the velvet chairs. There seemed to be a great deal of deliberation about placing the desks at the exact right angle for each team member, and the exact location of pencils and spare pencils and stacks of paper on the desks.

The screen above the chairs lit up, showing an enlarged view of the surface of each desk.

The crowd in the bleachers let out a collective "ahhh!"

Like that's exciting? KT thought.

"And now, for our home team, the Brecksville North Scholars . . . ," the announcer began.

We're not the Scholars! KT thought indignantly. *We're the Chieftains!*

But she could barely hear herself think in the roar of approval that came from the crowd behind her. Mom was tugging on her arm again, to get her to stand.

"Evangeline Marietta Rangel!" the announcer screamed.

Of course, KT thought.

Evangeline trotted toward the nearest desk. She was wearing shiny black little-girl shoes—were they called Mary Janes?—and argyle socks and a khaki skirt and an argyle vest.

Hideous, KT thought.

"Ebenezer Joseph Bashkov!" the announcer screamed.

Ebenezer? KT thought. *It's not Benjamin? Has that always been that poor kid's name?*

Ben stumbled out to his desk, his knobby knees revealed for all the world to see because the Brecksville North uniform for guys was khaki shorts and argyle socks and a blazer and argyle tie. But he was pumping his scrawny arms and beaming—like a football player after scoring the winning touchdown, like a basketball player after making an amazing slam dunk, like a baseball or softball player after batting in a four-run homer.

In the midst of all the cheering, Mom leaned forward and said to Mrs. Bashkov, "You must be so proud."

"Oh, we are," Mrs. Bashkov said reverently. "We are."

"Molly Isabel O'Toole!" the announcer called. "Alexandra Suzanne DeVries!"

Traitors, KT thought.

Molly and Lex strutted to their desks with the same easy confidence they showed walking up to bat in softball. They high-fived each other, then high-fived Ben and Evangeline. The crowd cheered louder.

"What if Max isn't starting?" KT heard Mom hiss frantically to Dad. "What if the coach doesn't give him the playing time he deserves?"

"He'll start. He'll start," Dad hissed back.

"And, finally, Maxwell Charles Sutton!" the announcer screamed.

"Ooh, baby!" some girl behind KT shrieked in the midst of all the other cheers.

Sick, KT thought.

Max walked away from his second-string teammates, who were resignedly sitting down on a bench at the other side of the room. He wobbled slightly, and KT had an odd flashback, remembering video of him as a baby learning how to walk. He moved just as tentatively now. His face looked pale and clammy, and he had his lips pinched tightly together, as if he was telling himself, *Don't vomit. Whatever you do, don't vomit.* He managed only the feeblest of waves at the crowd.

It figures, KT thought. *The world reverses, nerds are suddenly cool, and my brother still looks and acts pathetic.*

"All rise for the singing of 'The Star-Spangled Banner,'" the announcer said.

Both math teams sprang to their feet. The crowd in the bleachers was already standing, but everyone straightened up, snapping to respectful attention. Hundreds of hands pressed solemnly and patriotically against hundreds of chests.

The announcer must have pressed a button somewhere, because the first strains of the national anthem rolled out of the speakers: "O-oh, say, can you see? By the dawn's early light . . ."

It was this, finally, that was too much for KT to bear.

In her mind, "The Star-spangled Banner" properly belonged to sporting events, and the last lines—" . . . o'er the land of the free, and the home of the brave"—absolutely, positively had to be followed by the words "Play ball!"

What was the announcer going to say now? "Do math!"?

"No," KT moaned. "No, that's . . ."

Mr. and Mrs. Bashkov both turned around and peered at her with a mix of worry and annoyance. Several other people down the row turned and looked too. Mom's hand clamped down on KT's arm once again.

But KT yanked her arm away. She shoved her way through the crowd in front of her.

"I've got to go," she said over her shoulder, in the vague direction of Mom and Dad. "I'm . . . sick. I can't stay here."

She hit the floor and took off running. She smashed through the doors from the library into the empty hallway outside. She stood against the wall, panting hard.

Neither Mom nor Dad came after her.

Chapter Twelv3

KT had always thought the worst feeling in the world was being stuck on the bench during a close game, when you couldn't do a thing to help your team.

She'd been wrong.

It was infinitely worse to stand cowering in an empty hallway, outside a huge, important game that the whole town seemed to have shown up for—and have it not be her game or her sport or even her reality.

It was incalculably worse not to even have a team.

This is just a dream, she told herself. *A nightmare. It couldn't possibly be real.*

But didn't dreams usually end right about the time you figured out they were dreams?

She pinched her arm—nearly hard enough to draw blood—and still she didn't wake up. The sign staring at her from across the hall still said *ALL OUR NUMBERS ADD UP—YOUR TEAM IS AN INCORRECT CALCULATION!* Just as girls now seemed to think guys like Ben and Max were hot, maybe that passed for a clever taunt in this world.

It's not a different world, KT corrected herself. *It's just . . . just . . .*

She didn't have words to explain it to herself. She couldn't get her mind around any of this. But did she actually have to understand this place to be able to get out of it?

She slammed her shoulder against the wall, just in case it was possible to break through, to get back to the real world that way. This was how KT barreled through first basemen who got in her way, catchers who got in her way—*anything* that got in her way.

The wall was perfectly solid. It *seemed* real.

Hitting it just made KT's shoulder hurt.

Like last night, at the Rysdale Invitational . . .

Just thinking about the Rysdale Invitational—thinking about the real world containing something as amazing as the Rysdale Invitational—made KT's whole body ache with loss.

Down the hall, a burst of cheering spilled out of the library, followed by a collective groan of disappointment and another exultant cheer.

The thrill of victory and the agony of defeat, KT thought.

She couldn't stand listening to the crowd noise anymore. Not when it was for math. Not when it was a reminder that everything she loved had vanished.

She edged farther down the hall. A door stood partly open, an electrical cord winding from an outlet in the hallway to a vacuum cleaner just inside the classroom. It looked like maybe the janitor had walked away from his job to go watch the math competition.

But that's ridiculous, KT thought. *Why would a janitor care about a math competition?*

Why would anyone?

She forgot this line of reasoning when she noticed what else was in this classroom: desks. Computers.

See? See? she told herself. *There are normal classrooms! So there should be normal sports, too!*

Then she saw the words on the classroom bulletin board: *WELCOME TO AC ED!*

Ac ed, KT thought. *Academic education. Has to be this world's answer to phys ed. It's the nearest room to the library, just as my phys ed classroom was the nearest room to the gym.*

But she sat down at one of the computers and turned it on.

This time she didn't bother looking for the Rysdale Invitational site, the "Bring softball back to the Olympics" Facebook page, or any of the other sites she normally had bookmarked on her computer at home. She did a simple Google search, typing in one word:

SOFTBALL

A short list of responses came up. KT clicked blindly on the first one. It was only a definition.

SOFTBALL: a little-known game, rarely played, involving bats and balls and bases

In a panic, KT hit the red-squared *X* at the top of the page. She sat still, breathing hard.

Little-known? Rarely played? Nooooo . . .

She decided to start slow, maybe with sports she didn't care about so much. She Googled soccer, tennis, football, basketball, rugby, lacrosse. Field hockey. Water polo. And it seemed like people still played these sports some in this version of the world.

Okay, rarely, KT told herself, forcing herself to face facts. *So . . . kids spend all day in school doing sports conditioning and almost never actually play the games?*

She guessed it was kind of like how, in the real world, students spent so much time drilling and drilling to be ready for the state tests but almost never did lab experiments or field trips or other activities that kids who actually liked school might call fun.

Well, who cares? I don't need a lot of people playing the same sport as me, KT thought. *I don't need hundreds of people cheering me on. I just need softball.*

She took a deep breath and Googled "softball" again. She added a second word: "leagues." After a moment, she added four more: "in the United States."

The search results came up.

The nearest softball league was four hundred miles away.

"There you are," a voice said from the doorway.

KT looked up. It was Dad.

"Max had a terrible game," Dad said. "I think you rattled him, running out like that."

KT shrugged.

"Sorry," she said. Even to her own ears, her voice sounded sullen and sulky.

"What has gotten into you?" Dad asked. "We've never

had this kind of problem with you before. You get such good grades . . ."

KT remembered Molly and Lex laughing about how if you got straight As, teachers and parents acted like you should be a saint. She'd never really thought about it before, but Molly and Lex probably did get straight As.

In the real world.

Probably in this one too. They were lucky. They could be happy both places.

"What are you doing in here?" Dad asked.

"Looking for people like me," KT said, and somehow all the pain she'd been holding back throbbed in her voice.

"Oh, princess," Dad said. He eased the door almost all the way shut and came over and wrapped his arms around KT.

"I'm not anyone's princess," KT said fiercely. Dad hadn't called her that since she was four. Nobody called pitchers "princess."

She pushed him away and pointed to the softball-league information frozen on the screen.

"Will you take me to this?" KT asked.

Dad looked at the screen, then did a double take.

"That's hundreds of miles away!" he said. "You know we couldn't do that!"

"You'd do it if it were Max's math team," KT said, the sulkiness back in her voice. She didn't know this for a fact, but she couldn't say, *You drove me that far in the real world for softball.*

Dad sighed.

"Max's math . . . has a future to it," Dad said. "He's young yet, but if he plays as well as I think he can in high school, he'll get a full-ride college scholarship out of it. Maybe he'll even go pro. The sky's the limit for Max."

"But not for me?" KT wailed.

"Now, now," Dad said, patting her shoulder. "You'll have a very . . . stable life. Easier than Max's, in a lot of ways. You'll be a good employee someday out in the work world. Of course, maybe if you start playing some sort of ac now, maybe you can still have a better high-school experience . . ."

A sly note crept into his voice, and KT thought maybe this was an argument Mom and Dad had been making with her alternate-world self for a long time.

Just like they keep bugging Max in the real world to start playing some sort of sport, KT thought.

"*You* didn't play acs in high school!" KT protested. "You played sports! Cross-country! Wrestling! Baseball!"

"KT, you know that's a lie!" Dad scolded her. "You know I got varsity letters in three acs—mathletics, chemademics, and geography find. Though, I have to admit, I was *lousy* at geo. There just weren't that many other guys at my school who wanted to go out for that team."

That was how he used to talk about cross-country.

KT blinked, doing something like translation in her head.

All those stories Dad always tells about his high-school career, how he was "this close" to a baseball scholarship at UCLA, and how that's why it would be doubly sweet to see me get a softball scholarship—it's all flipped around in this world. It's acs he was good at, acs he almost got a scholarship for, acs he wants to see his kid do better at than he could do himself . . .

And it flipped around so Dad wanted Max to succeed, not KT.

"You only care about Max," KT accused bitterly.

Dad let out another deep, heavy sigh.

"We're back to that, are we?" he complained. "Your mother said you were just jealous of Max."

"No, I'm not!" KT protested.

"Then stop acting like it!" Dad said. "Stop whining! You want people to play some silly game with? Then find them right here in Brecksville! Organize a league yourself!"

KT opened her mouth to protest the word "silly." Then she shut it. Dad was being mean, but KT had dealt with plenty of mean coaches and teammates and opponents over the years. It didn't help to taunt back.

Especially when he'd actually had a good idea.

KT Sutton, pitcher, did not sit around moaning and groaning and complaining when things didn't go her way. She *made* them turn around. She'd snatched wins away from stronger, faster, better opponents. She'd pulled off come-from-behind victories when her team was losing by as many as ten runs.

Maybe the way to get back to the real world was by making this one actually bearable.

All she had to do was create her own softball team.

Chapter Thirte3n

KT and Dad met up with Mom and Max in the school lobby, in front of the school trophy case. The engraved desks still hung near the top of the case where the jerseys belonged. And KT saw now that the trophies were all for acs, not sports: the three acs Dad had named—mathletics, chemademics, and geo find—as well as historia, poetry slam, write-a-thon, bio bash, translatOr and something called spelldown.

Never mind, KT told herself. *I'm still going to have softball.*

"You are *so* deep in trouble," Mom said, glaring at KT. "We'll talk about this later."

Other kids and families walked by, dutifully calling out, "Good game, Max!" Mom pasted on a fake smile and turned around to face them.

"There's always next year against Winchester!" she called out.

Max's team must have lost.

KT glanced at her brother. He didn't look like he'd added up a couple of numbers wrong. He looked like he'd been tackled. Possibly by an entire football team at once.

Max's face was even more colorless than it had been at the beginning of the competition. His hair stuck up all over the place, as if he'd been tugging on it, trying to pull answers out of his brain. His fingernails were chewed down to the quick.

And—worst of all—his bottom lip was trembling.

"Shake it off," KT told him. "Buck up."

She actually meant that in a friendly way. "Shake it off" was what Coach Mike had told her that time she'd been hit in the chest by a line drive so fast she hadn't had a chance to get her glove behind it. When bad things happened, you did just have to shake them off and keep going. That was why KT was going to shake off this crazy mixed-up world by starting her own softball team. Maybe an entire league.

But Mom grabbed KT's arm and yanked her off to the side, out of the path of the disappointed crowd leaving the mathletics competition.

"If you utter the words 'it's only a game' or 'it's only math—it's not like it's something important like school,' so help me, you will be grounded the rest of your life," Mom said.

"I wasn't saying that!" KT protested.

But—had she said it before in this alternate world? Just like Max had said "it's only a game" to KT in the real world?

"Just stay away from your brother," Mom said. She glanced back toward Dad and Max, still waiting by the trophy case, and her voice turned lighter and kinder. "Max, when we get to the car, you can sit in the front with Dad, to go over your strategies for your next game. And do you want to go to Applebee's for dinner?"

No! KT thought. *Applebee's is where Mom and Dad always take me to cheer up after a loss!*

But she kept her mouth shut.

Softball, she told herself. *Just think about how to organize your softball team.*

She did notice that Max wasn't jumping at the chance to go to Applebee's.

"I just want to go home," he moaned.

"All right, buddy," Dad said in an even voice. "Maybe we'll order pizza."

They walked out to the car. Mom and Dad still had to run interference with people calling out to Max. They were almost like his bodyguards.

KT trailed three or four paces behind.

I'll re-friend my entire club softball team on Facebook, she thought. *I'll send them invitations to join me in this new softball league. And I'll send invitations to everyone who was on the seventh-grade school softball team last year—no, everyone I remember even trying out. I remember a lot of last year's eighth graders, too—I can send them messages as well.*

She got in the car behind Dad and slid as far over from Mom as she could.

I know who I'll invite from this year's seventh graders too, KT thought. *And maybe there are some sixth graders who would be good. . . .*

In the front seat Dad was saying, "and Max, you were the first one who figured out to solve for x in that train problem. I was watching everyone's screen. You just didn't buzz in with the answer fast enough."

"I never want to do that again," Max moaned.

"There's the spirit!" Dad said. "Take a vow: 'I'll never get beat on the buzzer when I have the right answer first.' Even if it's your own teammate buzzing in faster, you don't want that!"

"No," Max said, "that's not what I meant. I meant I never want to be in another math competition in my life."

"Maxwell Charles! Don't say things like that!" Mom cried.

Dad had been starting to pull out into the street, but now he slammed on the brake. KT's head hit the seat in front of her. Dad lined up the car with the curb once more and put it back in park. He turned to face Max.

"I am not raising a quitter," Dad said sternly.

"Why not?" Max muttered. "Why shouldn't I quit something I hate?"

"Max, you have a great talent," Mom chimed in from the backseat. "An incredible talent. Very few people at your school are capable of doing what you do."

"I felt like I was going to puke the whole time I was up there," Max said. "Mr. Horace told me a hundred times, 'Max, we're counting on you. Max, we're counting on you.' I don't want people counting on me! I don't want people watching me! Especially not when I'm doing math!"

"Max, you had one bad game," Dad said, soothingly. "That's no reason to give up a promising career."

"Career?" Max said. "Career? I'm twelve years old! I don't have a career!"

"If he's that miserable, you should let him quit," KT said.

"That's it! You are grounded for two weeks!" Mom said, whipping around and pointing an accusing finger at KT.

"Just for trying to help my brother?" KT wailed.

She'd never been grounded before in her life. What if that meant she couldn't start her softball team for another two weeks? She hadn't gone an entire two weeks without playing softball since she was eight.

Of course, she really hadn't been trying to help her brother. She'd mostly just wanted Mom and Dad to stop talking and drive home, so she could start sending out messages about starting a softball league.

Dad turned off the car. He turned sideways in his seat so he could face the entire rest of the family at once.

"Everyone needs to calm down," he said. He took a deep breath. "KT, I would like to take you at your word and try to believe that you were, indeed, trying to help your brother. We'll talk about the grounding later. And Max, I understand that you had a bad game. I remember what it's like to feel like you've let your team down, let your coach down, let your family down. But *quitting is not the answer.*"

KT wanted so badly to say, *Why not? Who cares?* But she didn't want to be grounded for three weeks.

"Max," Mom said in a tremulous voice. "You have so much potential. Why would you throw away such a golden opportunity?"

She sounded like she was on the verge of tears.

Dad cleared his throat, sounding a little emotional himself.

"When I failed to get that mathletics scholarship at UCLA," he said, "I knew exactly what that meant. All my dreams—crushed. All my possibilities—evaporated like so much morning dew."

This was a very, very strange version of Dad. In the real world he only talked about sports. Even when he talked about other things, sports crept in. His coworkers were "in a first-down situation" or some project was "a slam dunk" or some other company had done "an end run" around his.

"Losing that scholarship," Dad continued in a somber voice, "I knew I was in for a lifetime of hard physical labor."

"Hard physical labor?" KT cried. "Dad, you're an accountant!" Dad gave her a rueful smile.

"Thanks for the vote of confidence, sweetie, but you know that's only a hobby," Dad said sadly.

"Ha-ha," KT started to say, because sometimes back in the real world Dad would joke that being an accountant was just a hobby— his real job was driving KT to softball practices and games.

But maybe—maybe in this world he's serious? KT thought in amazement. *If school and sports flipped around, does that mean adults' jobs changed too? Accounting is what people do for fun and . . . what exactly does he do in his job in this world?*

"You spend your workday exercising," Max said in a flat, expressionless voice.

"You know we do," Mom said bitterly. "You know your father and I are on treadmills all day long."

KT had heard Mom refer to her job in an insurance office as a treadmill before, but what if she actually meant that literally? What if jogging was Mom's whole job now?

"But—," KT started to say. Then she realized she couldn't ask what she really wanted to. "But . . . isn't that fun?" she finished lamely.

"*You* would think so," Mom said. The bitterness in her voice was almost overwhelming.

"We hope you love your job when you get out into the work world," Dad said, back to his soothing tones. "We hope both our children will be very happy in their chosen careers. And that means developing your talents to their full potential. Which begins right now. Max, you can't take it easy at this point in your life and expect to just catch up later on."

"What if I don't want to catch up?" Max asked. "What if I just want to . . . hang out? Be myself?"

"Oh, Max, mathletics *is* you," Mom said. "You are a mathletics champion. It's like your coach told us way back in second grade: 'Max's mind is made for math.' Do you know how proud we were when we heard that?"

KT couldn't help herself. She snorted.

Mom snapped her attention back to KT.

"Young lady!" she began.

"I'm sorry! I'm sorry!" KT apologized, spreading her hands out flat, a gesture of innocence. "I was just . . . breathing." She wanted to add, *I'm allowed to do that much in this family, aren't I?* But she thought better of it. "Maybe . . . maybe you want to have this conversation with Max in private? Maybe, so I don't get into any more trouble, I should just walk home on my own?"

Mom gave a quick glance out the window. KT realized she was looking to see who would notice if they let KT out. Evidently nobody important was around, because Mom narrowed her eyes at KT and said, "Go ahead."

KT opened the car door. She was surprised to see that her legs were shaking as she stood up. She made her way to the sidewalk.

Don't they care about me at all? she wondered.

She heard the electronic sound behind her that meant someone was rolling down a car window. She turned back, and Dad had his head halfway out.

"Turns out we are going to Applebee's," he said. "You want us to bring something back for you, or do you just want to grab something at home?"

Okay, they care enough to offer me food, KT thought. *Cold food, after they're done eating. Big whoop.*

"No, thanks," KT said, with what she hoped was great dignity. "I'll make myself a sandwich."

She wanted to whirl back around and stalk away, but she watched Dad's face just a moment longer, willing him to say, *Oh, you don't have to do that! Here—hop in the car! We'll go through the drive-through at Wendy's for you first thing, drop you off at home, and* then *we'll take Max out!*

Instead Dad said coldly, "Suit yourself."

KT looked away from Dad. She didn't mean it to, but her gaze fell on Max, just for an instant. He was staring straight back at KT, his face more pinched and pale and desperate than ever. It had been years since KT had been the least bit interested in what Max might be thinking, but in that moment she felt like she could read his mind. He was thinking: *No, please! Don't go!*

KT spun on her heel and started walking briskly away.

Right, Max, KT thought. *You just want me around so Mom and Dad will yell at me instead of lecturing you. Forget it!*

She straightened her shoulders, broadened her stride. No way was she going to let Mom and Dad and Max see how upset she was.

Keep your head down and pitch, she told herself. *Walk. Plan your softball league. Use it to get back to the real world. Back to the real world where . . .*

She almost didn't let herself finish the thought. But KT Sutton, pitcher, was no coward. There was no room in softball for cowards.

Back to the real world where your parents actually love you.

Chapter F0urte3n

KT was busy that evening. After assembling and eating a dry, tasteless peanut-butter sandwich, she put all of Max's stupid trophies back in the shrine—her first step toward getting back into Mom and Dad's good graces so that maybe they'd cut back her grounding sentence. She took a shower, then sent Facebook messages to every single person within a fifty-mile radius she could remember playing softball with or against in the past six years: "Want to have the most fun in your life? Want to use the skills you learn in school for something that's actually worthwhile? Join my softball league! If you're interested, let me know!"

She sat back in her chair and watched the screen. She hit the refresh symbol.

Nothing.

Silly, it's hasn't even been a full minute, she chided herself. *Give them some time to let the idea sink in. It's not like they know about the real world.*

Wait—what if some of them did know about the real world? For all KT could tell, maybe her whole club softball team had been zapped into this bizarre land at once, all of them suddenly living alternate lives. Or maybe some of her friends from school knew about the real world, just not the friends she'd talked to today. How could KT find out if they knew? How would they know that KT knew too?

KT stared at her computer screen for a moment. Then she began to type out a second message to her whole club team: "I'm thinking of calling my softball league the Rysdale Invitational, Part Two. What do you think of that? Does it remind you of anything?"

That should do it.

She came up with similar coded messages for girls from school, girls from previous teams, girls she'd met at softball camps or played against. "Maybe we'll all eat a dozen hot dogs afterward!" she wrote to Letty Rodriguez, a tiny girl who'd astonished the rest of KT's fourth-grade team by polishing off that many hot dogs at the end-of-season cookout.

"Maybe we can all use glitter-covered gloves!" she wrote to Hanna Ding, who'd had an unfortunate accident involving her catcher's mitt and her little sister's craft project right before a big game in sixth grade.

"We'll only hire bald umpires," she wrote to Keshia Washington, a girl she'd hung out with at softball camps three years in a row. They'd shared a running joke about how none of the umpires in the school leagues had any hair.

KT lifted her hands from the keyboard. So many memories. So many inside jokes, so many disasters, so many triumphs. Were they all still true if nobody but KT remembered?

She rubbed her eyes, and put her fingers back on the keys. She typed: "Please tell me you remember too. Please."

She didn't send that message. She left it on the screen, the cursor still blinking. She clicked back to her Facebook news feed and hit the refresh button.

Nothing.

Again.

Nothing.

Again.

Nothing.

She heard the garage door, then Mom and Dad and Max talking downstairs. She should go down, watch some ESPN with Dad, wait until his team was winning, and then, during a commercial break, suggest that maybe it really wasn't necessary to ground KT for two whole weeks.

She heard the TV coming on, an overly loud announcer's voice calling out breathlessly, "Which of these poets will make it to the semifinals?" before someone—probably Dad—set it back to a normal volume.

Poets? KT thought. *Oh, yeah, there's probably no ESPN anymore, either.*

Of course. Something else she loved that had vanished from this world.

She heard someone climbing the stairs, and quickly reached over and turned out her light. She couldn't face talking to Dad or Mom or Max anymore tonight. She sat perfectly still in the dark, barely daring to breathe. The footsteps paused outside KT's door, then moved on.

KT let out her held breath, and tiptoed over to her bed and lay down. She would go to sleep. Maybe that was all she needed to do to escape this world. Maybe she'd made things more complicated than they needed to be. She would go to sleep, and when she woke up, she'd have her real world back. She'd have softball back. She'd even know the outcome of the Rysdale Invitational.

She closed her eyes, and some of her fears from the morning came back to her.

Hospital, beeping monitors, concerned voices . . .

She fought back with her visualization coach's best strategies.

I'm on the field. I'm pitching a no-hitter. I'm back in the world where everyone loves softball. Mom and Dad are proud of me again. This whole day is barely even a memory. I have softball back. I have softball back. I have softball back. . . .

She fell asleep whispering those words.

Chapter Fifteen

KT woke to Mom standing over her bed, the early-morning sunlight glowing around her.

Yes! KT thought. *It must be the regular world, back again! Why else would Mom bother coming in to talk to me?*

"About last night . . . ," Mom said, sitting down on the edge of KT's bed.

"Yes?" KT said, springing up eagerly. This must be the way yesterday was supposed to go. All that weirdo-world stuff must have been a dream. Mom was going to say, *We were so proud of you at the Rysdale Invitational,* or maybe, *We've already heard from the first scout from a top-tier high school club team,* or maybe . . .

"Dad and I were talking after you went to bed," Mom continued. "We really need you to be more supportive of Max."

"What?" KT exclaimed. Behind Mom, KT could see the blank space on her wall where the Olympic softball pictures were supposed to be. Pretending to stretch, she craned her neck and looked at the bulletin board over her bed.

It held report cards, not softball goals.

KT sank back into her pillows.

"You heard me," Mom said grimly. "Though you may not realize it, Max looks up to you. You're his older sister. This new attitude of his, not wanting to play mathletics—he must be paying too much attention to your opinions. You've put doubts in his mind, sent him into crisis."

Are you nuts? KT wanted to scream at her mother. *Max messes up, Max is too lazy to work hard—and it's my fault? How is that fair?*

She pressed her lips together.

You can't say what you really think, she reminded herself. *Not unless you want Mom to ground you even longer.*

She swallowed hard.

"I won't say anything bad to Max about math," KT said. "If you un-ground me."

Mom frowned, deliberating.

"Deal," she said.

KT gaped at her mother.

Geez, Mom, I guess you never took debate class in school— er, I mean, you never did an ac teaching negotiating skills, she thought. *You caved a million times faster than I expected.*

Unless—what if Mom cared only about keeping Max in mathletics? What if she didn't care at all about teaching KT a lesson by grounding her?

It was weird to feel so dejected about not being punished.

Mom and Dad almost never punished me in the real world, KT thought. *There was never time, because I was always playing softball.*

And it would be that way again.

"Can you leave now so I can get dressed?" KT asked Mom, not bothering to keep the rudeness out of her voice.

As soon as Mom was gone, KT went over to her laptop. She'd left it on overnight, almost as if she'd expected the answers to come in faster that way. She had three messages, one from Bree on her club team, one from Keshia Washington, and one from a sixth grader from school she'd seen playing softball once at the park.

"Who are you?" said Bree's message.

"Do I know you?" asked Keshia's.

"My big sister says hanging out with you will make me really, really unpopular in middle school," the sixth grader's said.

KT sat staring at the sixth grader's message for a long time.

"Shake it off," she whispered to herself.

She deleted the sixth grader's message, and deleted the sixth grader's name from the group she'd assembled for sending out messages.

I'm not grounded anymore, she reminded herself. *We can start playing softball immediately.*

She remembered that some of the girls lived far away and would have to make arrangements for someone to drive them.

Saturday, she told herself. *I can survive until Saturday.*

She typed out a new message to send to the whole group:

"You may or may not know me, but I heard that you are someone who does really well in school but might be a little bored by it. That's how I am too. I know about a game called softball that I think you will love. Want to play? Come to Ridgestone Park in Brecksville at ten a.m., Saturday, February 13, for lots of fun!"

She started to type, "Don't forget to bring your own glove and bat," but then she remembered, *It's weirdo world. What if no one has gloves and bats?* She went down to the garage, to the expanded section at the back that her dad always jokingly referred to as "KT's sporting-goods store." In the real world she had a whole lineup of bats, dating back to her third-grade version. And she had racks of cleats, some almost destroyed, some in the "still being broken in" category. And she had baskets full of softballs, three separate customized sports bags, a spare backup glove along with a collection of outgrown gloves, a similar lineup of old and new batting helmets, and a lifesize pitching mate to practice with when Dad wasn't available to catch her blistering throws.

She turned the light on and peered around Mom's car to see what lay there now.

One pair of cleats.

One old glove.

One small basket of balls.

And, incredibly enough, the pitching mate.

No bats.

Well, at least I have the cleats and balls and a spare glove, she told herself, trying to put a positive spin on things. *If I still have my regular glove, probably other girls have gloves too. Maybe for that class at school where people throw balls all the time?*

She hugged the sturdy frame of the pitching mate like it was a long-lost friend. But weirdo world was getting into her brain. KT had probably gotten the pitching mate for her eleventh birthday, just like in the real world. But in this world, getting it wouldn't have been like Mom and Dad saying to her,

Yeah! We believe in your pitching talent! You're going to be great, and we're going to do everything we can to help you! It would have been like a little kid in the real world asking for a dictionary or a collected set of Shakespeare plays or a graphing calculator. It would have been something Mom and Dad kind of wondered at, maybe even laughed at with their friends: *You'll never guess what KT wanted for her birthday!* But secretly maybe they'd worried: *If we get her this, will she just become odder? Why doesn't she like what all the other kids like? What's wrong with her?*

"Stop it," KT told herself aloud. The words echoed in the too-empty garage. "Focus on organizing your softball game for Saturday."

She ran back upstairs and clicked over to eBay on her laptop. It was true—you really could find anything on eBay. Even in this pathetic, practically softball-less world, she had her choice of a dozen softball bats. She clicked on the next-day-delivery shipping option, but that made the price go up by sixty dollars. She opened another screen to check how much money she had on her debit card. What if Mom and Dad were stingier with their money here than in the real world?

She had roughly three hundred dollars more than she should have.

Oh, right, she thought. *I guess Mom and Dad still pay for As on report cards, even in bizarre world.*

At least there were some advantages.

But it's not worth losing softball, she told herself quickly, just in case her thoughts had any connection to getting out of this world. *I still want softball back!*

"KT! Have you had breakfast yet?" Mom yelled from

downstairs. "The bus is going to be here in five minutes!"

"Coming!" KT yelled back.

She hastily finished her order and sent out a quick message to everyone on her potential softball team: "I will have one bat and one spare glove for Saturday, but bring any softball equipment you can find, just in case."

She rushed down the stairs and grabbed an energy bar and chugged some milk in the kitchen.

"KT! The bus is here *now*!" Mom yelled from near the front door. "Max is already on it!"

"I'm there!" KT said, running out of the kitchen. She raced past Mom, out the door, across the yard.

This is actually perfect, KT thought. *I didn't see Max all morning. I avoided him entirely.*

How else could she manage to avoid telling him mathletics was stupid? How else could she avoid getting grounded, and losing softball all over again?

Chapter Sixteen

The days passed slowly.

Every morning KT woke up thinking, *Maybe it was all a dream! Maybe this will be the day the real world's back!* But each morning she was less and less surprised to open her eyes to blank walls where Olympic pictures should have been, to report cards on her bulletin board in place of her list of softball goals.

Every night, falling asleep, she had the same flash of imagining some awful outcome to the Rysdale Invitational. Sometimes it was a sense of being in another place, in another condition: *hospital, traction, full-body cast, in a wheelchair, on crutches . . .* Other times it was more of a listing of injuries she didn't want to have: *Broken bone? Dislocated shoulder? ACL tear? Concussion?*

She countered those fears with the same thought every night: *The last thing I remember at the Rysdale Invitational, I was throwing a ball. How could something go that wrong, throwing a ball?*

Her mind dodged searching for answers. She always shifted to planning for her softball game or league on Saturday instead.

How many girls will show up? she wondered. *Will we have enough for just two teams, or enough for more of a tournament?* She knew she'd have to organize things quickly—softball girls didn't like standing around waiting to play. She made up imaginary rosters in her head, based on which girls she thought would show up.

At school, she stuck to her policy of "Keep your head down and pitch." She savored stretching her legs in the treadmill class, throwing balls in the pitching class, feeling the pull of her muscles in weight lifting. Really, the classes would have been great—certainly better than the usual boring worksheets and homework and droning lectures—if only she'd had friends around her instead of kids who gave her sideways glances and whispered about her behind her back. And if all that working out had been leading to something, not just exercise for the sake of exercise.

It will, KT thought. *I'll get to play softball on Saturday.*

The only class she didn't like was ac ed, which was indeed academic—every subject from regular eighth grade crammed into one class. The teacher, Mr. Stone, who was a science teacher in the real world, seemed to assume that everyone played an ac, so he didn't teach anything. He just asked a bunch of hard questions about topics KT had never heard of.

KT avoided talking to Mr. Stone. She avoided talking to any of the other teachers too, even the ones who seemed to be trying to be friendly.

I'm already a pariah, KT thought, when Ms. Alvarez, the

weight-lifting teacher, seemed to want to engage KT in a long one-on-one conversation about the best gripping technique. *Does she think I want to make things worse by acting like a teacher is my best friend?*

She especially avoided all the teachers who'd had strange conversations with her the first day: Mr. Huck and Mr. Horace and Mrs. Whitbourne.

She didn't have to work very hard at avoiding the other kids, because they mostly avoided her. In fact the only time anyone her own age talked to her was Wednesday afternoon after they'd had a pop quiz in throwing class. "Pop quiz" in this world evidently meant standing on a line and firing ten balls in a row at the target. Mrs. Sanchez called out a type of pitch with every one: "Fastball!" Curveball!" "Changeup!"

KT had to admit, this was a lot more fun than true-or-false. *So why don't they have batters standing there instead of a stupid old target?* she wondered. *That would be even better!*

But as soon as the quiz was over, two kids came rushing over to KT. One of them, Anthony Seitz, had been the starting quarterback of the eighth-grade football team in the real world. The other, Celia Waters, had been big into volleyball.

"What'd you get?" Anthony asked.

"Bet she got a higher score than you," Celia teased.

KT shrugged.

"A hundred," she said, and resisted adding, *Are you kidding? That was easy! I could have aced that test when I was nine!*

Celia punched Anthony's bulging bicep.

"Told you so!" she cried.

"Ah, man, couldn't you just get a ninety-nine once, give

the rest of us a chance to catch up?" Anthony complained. "I would have had a hundred too, if Mrs. Sanchez hadn't stuttered on that last changeup. I thought sure she was going to say curveball!"

"Poor baby," Celia mocked him. "Did your average in this class actually fall to ninety-nine-point-eight?"

Great, KT thought. *The jocks in this world are the ones who are grade-obsessed. And they can't even do math!*

Celia seemed to be counting up her own score on her fingers.

But the way Celia and Anthony were joking around together . . . it was like they were friends. With each other, at least. Being good at school hadn't made them into outcasts.

"Hey, how about if I sit with you at lunch and tell you my secret strategy?" KT asked.

Celia and Anthony exchanged glances.

"Sorry," Anthony said. "We're sitting with our chemademics team. I don't think you'd be interested in what we're talking about."

Chemademics. Of course. Anthony had to point out that he wasn't just some grade-obsessed jock. He played an ac, too. He was cool.

But how could bonehead Anthony Seitz know anything about chemistry? KT wondered. *Unless . . . maybe he was just faking his boneheadedness in the real world? Acting like he thought jocks were supposed to act?*

It was too confusing. Who was the real Anthony? Who around her had showed their real self in the real world, and who was more their real self here?

KT had a lot of time to think about this during lunch that

day. It was just her and her iPod and phone. She pretended not to care, and hunched over the iPod and phone acting like she had dozens of massively important texts and messages to send out.

"It would be great if you let me know if you're going to be able to come or not on Saturday," she messaged her entire list during lunch. "Let me know what position you'd like to play, too. That way I can start planning team rosters ahead of time."

But she didn't really expect everyone to answer. That was, like, RSVPing. Kids just didn't do that.

At least the bat arrived from UPS on Wednesday afternoon. KT immediately took the package up to her room, tore off the wrapping, and stood there in the middle of the floor in batting stance. She swung.

A little too heavy at the end, she decided, swinging again to double-check. *Not as good as my bat in the real world. But it'll do.*

It felt great just holding a bat, just crouching with it in batting position. She didn't think she could wait all the way to Saturday to actually use it. As soon as dinner was over that night, she turned to Dad.

"Would you help me with some . . . homework?" she asked.

Dad frowned.

"Does it have to be tonight?" he asked. "I was going to review some math strategies with Max after dinner."

Max had already had two hours of math practice right after school. He'd already had Mom and Dad fussing over him during the meal: "Are you getting enough protein to have enough energy to prep for Friday's game?" "You'll make sure to go to bed early tonight, won't you? You have to make sure you're rested up and your brain is sharp. I bet that was your problem Monday. You just aren't getting enough sleep."

"I guess I could help you, KT," Mom said reluctantly.

Mom was a terrible pitcher. Even in the real world.

"Okay," KT said, equally reluctant.

Having Mom pitch to her was better than having no one at all pitch to her until Saturday.

They went out in the backyard, KT lugging the bat and the basket of balls from the garage.

"You want me to throw to you?" Mom asked suspiciously. "And then . . . you'll catch the ball on the tip of that club thing?"

"It's called a bat, Mom," KT corrected. "And I'll hit the ball, not catch it. Throw the ball to me in about this area." She moved her hand around, showing Mom a rough version of a strike zone.

Mom frowned doubtfully, but tossed the ball. Like all Mom's throws, it was fit mostly for a kindergartner newly moving up from hitting off a tee. But KT swung at it anyway. The ball dribbled off into the grass at the bottom of the yard.

"You have to do this for pitching class?" Mom asked skeptically. "I don't remember this being in the curriculum."

"It's kind of . . . extra credit," KT said. "For a game called softball. I read about it online."

Mom shrugged, and threw another pitch.

This time KT swung so the bat and ball collided right at the bat's sweet spot. The ball went soaring up into the air, sailing across four neighbors' backyards.

"Home run," KT whispered to herself.

"KT!" Mom exclaimed. "You could have broken a window doing that!"

"No, no, I can control where I hit it," KT explained.

"That was control?" Mom asked. "KT, I don't think—"

"We can go to the park," KT offered quickly. "No windows will be in danger."

Mom shook her head.

"I've got three loads of laundry left to do tonight," she said. "This is just extra credit, right? I thought it was going to be something you had to do. I'm sure you've already got an A in this class. Probably even an A-plus."

"But—"

"KT, *no*," Mom said impatiently. She dropped the next ball back into the basket. "I don't have time for this."

Mom was already walking back toward the house. She slid open the patio door and disappeared inside.

KT did not like this world's version of Mom.

In the real world Mom was a terrible athlete too, but she was proud that I was so good at sports, KT thought. *Here, it's like she resents me getting good grades. Like she thinks I think I'm better than her.*

KT knew plenty of girls who fought constantly with their mothers. But she'd never been one of them.

She tried tossing the balls up in the air herself and batting them away.

"This one'll go into the Millers' yard, right by their patio," she whispered to herself, and hit it away. "This one will go over top of the Lurias' swing set."

But batting alone just made KT feel lonely. After a little while she gathered up all the balls and went back into the

house. She pointedly avoided walking past the dining-room table, where she could hear Dad saying to Max, "Now, if you take the square root, it could be positive or negative, right?"

She went straight up to her room and sent another message to her entire potential softball league: "You know, if you have any friends you think would want to play softball, you're welcome to bring them on Saturday too. They'll thank you for it, I just know it. You're going to love softball as much as I do! Your friends will too!"

On Friday afternoon Mom and Dad made KT go to Max's mathletics game once again.

"Mom, why?" KT asked, as Mom and Dad arrived home from work and began shouting out orders about getting ready. "I've got my own stuff to do."

Mom fixed KT with a stern glare.

"You're supposed to be supportive, remember?" Mom said.

"I kept my promise! I haven't said anything bad to Max all week about math!" KT protested.

Of course, she hadn't said *anything* to Max since Monday. She'd done a perfect job of avoiding him. It hadn't been too hard, since he was almost always away at math practices or coaching sessions. But she'd also avoided meeting his eye the one night they'd all had dinner together; she'd avoided going out for the bus at the same time as him; she'd even skipped brushing her teeth one night because she didn't want to cross paths with him walking to or from the bathroom.

"This is what we do as a family—we support each individual member of the family in every important endeavor," Mom said. "And that means you're coming to Max's game and you're going to cheer him on. Besides, I can tell you're just making excuses. I know you don't actually have anything else to do this afternoon."

KT really, really, really hated this world's version of Mom.

Don't say or do anything to get yourself grounded again, she told herself. *Remember, you get to have softball tomorrow.*

She repeated that to herself again and again to get through the national anthem. When the last notes, "of the brave," died out, she whispered to herself, "Play ball tomorrow. You'll get to play ball tomorrow."

Her words were drowned out by the roaring of the crowd. They stamped their feet and wolf-whistled and cheered. A line of cheerleaders came backflipping through the library doors, chanting, "Go, Scholars! Go, Scholars! Gooooooo, Scholars!" They finished with a string of cartwheels.

As far as KT could tell, cheerleaders in this world were almost identical to cheerleaders in the real world, except that their uniforms incorporated a bit more argyle and they all wore fake horn-rimmed glasses.

Great, that would be the one thing that stays the same, she thought. *Stupid old cheerleaders. They're like cockroaches— they could probably even survive nuclear war.*

"One, two, three, five, eight," the cheerleaders chanted. "Fibonacci freaks are great!"

Okay, maybe the cheers were a tiny bit different now.

They launched into another string of chanted numbers, and KT realized this was what Mom had as her ring tone.

Crazy, KT thought. *Totally nuts.*

But it turned out that the numbers were just a lead-in to a cheer that KT actually recognized: "Whyyyyy are you so blue? Is it because you are number two? We're number one!"

KT had to blink hard.

Of course her softball team was much too serious to do cheers now, but way back when she'd played in the Ponytail League in third grade, her coach had encouraged all the girls sitting on the bench to cheer their teammates on. KT had loved hearing her friends chanting that, louder and louder and louder, even as KT pitched strike after strike after strike. It was before KT had learned to focus properly, to block out everything but pitching. The cheers had made her pitch better back then. They had made her love her teammates even more.

Now she pulled out her iPod.

"I miss you guys so much," she wrote in a message to everyone she'd invited to play softball with her. "I can't wait to see you all tomorrow!"

"Put that away!" Mom said through clenched teeth, batting away the iPod with her hand. "Pay attention to the game!"

Don't get grounded, KT reminded herself. *Don't do anything to let anyone stop you from playing softball tomorrow.*

The mathletics game was starting now, and fortunately that made the cheerleaders shut up.

Max looked slightly less like he was on the verge of vomiting than he had before the last game. KT was still almost embarrassed for him when he buzzed in on the first question, even before he'd written anything down.

"Brecksville North, Maxwell," the announcer said.

"Um," Max said. He gulped. "Is it f-f-four?"

"It is indeed!" the announcer cried. "Excellent!"

Max just gulped again and smiled weakly, maybe like someone who'd been told he was going to be eaten alive by a pack of vicious lions but the death sentence had been delayed by a minute or two.

KT couldn't watch Max. She couldn't.

She discovered she couldn't watch her former friends Molly and Lex either, because they did so many things in mathletics the same way they played softball: Molly gripped her pencil way too tightly, just like she did with her bat; Lex tossed her hair over her shoulder before giving an answer the same way she always tossed her head after every pitch on the softball diamond.

Max's friend Ben was kind of funny to watch, because he stated every answer with absolute, perfect assurance—even when he was wrong.

But none of that really mattered, because the person who buzzed in almost every time was wacky little Evangeline Rangel. KT realized she'd never really seen Evangeline grin before, and it turned out that Evangeline had the type of grin that made you feel like you should be grinning just as much. She was fierce, too, slamming her pencil down and hitting the buzzer twice as hard as she needed to. After one particularly convoluted question that made KT's head hurt, Evangeline swatted the buzzer triumphantly and, grinning full-blast, cried out, "Forty-freaking-four!"

Evangeline is as feisty playing mathletics as I used to be playing softball, KT thought, and that "used to be" was like a dagger through her heart.

No! No! It's not "used to be"! I'm playing softball tomorrow! she told herself. *I'm getting softball back! I'm playing tomorrow and then, somehow, that will show this world who's boss, and everything will change back the right way!*

But that thought was enough to make it impossible for KT to watch Evangeline either. And when the cheerleaders jumped up for a time-out cheer in Evangeline's honor—"E [clap], E-V [clap], E-V-A-N-G-E-L and I-N-E [clap, clap]! She's our C-H-A-M-P and I-O-N [clap, clap, clap, clap]! Champion!"—that was like a dagger through KT's heart, too.

Why does she get her own cheer and her own game, and my game barely even exists in this world? KT wondered. *It's not fair!*

KT slipped into something like the zone she entered when she pitched—or maybe it was the flip side of that zone, because she just blurred out everything around her and did nothing. She stopped thinking; she let her hands fall loosely in her lap. She could have believed that she almost stopped existing. She was somewhat aware that the coach had put the second-string players in for the second round, and that Max's team fell far, far behind. In the third round, KT kind of noticed that the first string was back in, and Evangeline was answering a lot, but now every triumphant Evangeline grin just made KT feel more and more miserable, more and more adrift, more and more alone in the crowd.

And then Mom was clutching KT's arm.

"It's sudden death!" she hissed. "They're tied! I can't stand it! Everything comes down to this last question!"

The library was absolutely quiet, as if no one even dared to breathe.

"If Bob pays a quarter for an apple and a banana," the announcer began, in the same serious, hushed voice that golf announcers used in the real world, "and twenty cents for a banana and a pear, and twenty-one cents for an apple and a pear, how much would it cost Bob to buy just one of each fruit?"

Max buzzed in immediately.

Idiot! KT thought. *His coach and Mom and Dad are going to kill him for hitting the buzzer by mistake at a time like this!*

Max didn't even look like he'd realized he'd made a mistake.

"Oh," he said dreamily, like there weren't hundreds of people hanging onto his every word. "That's not as tricky as it sounds. You just add up all the numbers to get two of each fruit, and divide that in half. So it's . . ." He blinked, almost sleepily. "Thirty-three. Thirty-three cents."

"Yes," the announcer said.

The library exploded with screams and clapping and— from the opposing team—disappointed wails. People shot off streamers around KT; they cupped their hands into imitation bullhorns and made sounds like vuvuzelas. The cheerleaders jumped up and down and started the whole home side of the stands chanting, "Max! Max! Max! Max! Max!"

KT sat silently in the midst of all the hubbub and celebration. She slipped her iPod out of her pocket and sent another message out to her entire message list: "I can't wait to be around people who like the same things I like! People who know what's really important! It's only another fifteen hours! See you all tomorrow!"

Chapter Seventeen

Saturday morning dawned bright and crisp and clear. KT was up with the sun, doing stretches and sending out final reminder messages: "Today's the day! Don't forget to come to Ridgestone Park in Brecksville at ten a.m. for the great sport of softball!"

She packed up the old pillows she'd decided would be the best she could do for bases. She put those, the basket of balls, her two gloves, her cleats, and the bat in an old red wagon she'd found still in the garage from when she and Max were little. She went back upstairs and tried to decide what to wear.

It's not like I expect anyone to actually have uniforms, but it'd be nice if everyone on the same team wore the same color, she thought.

She sent out another message to everyone: "Bring a couple different colors of T-shirts as spares, so you can match your teammates."

In the real world KT had a great collection of softball-themed

T-shirts: a pink one saying (SOFTBALL) DIAMONDS ARE A GIRL'S BEST FRIEND, a black one saying, YEAH, I THROW LIKE A GIRL. SCARED YET? and drawers full of commemorative T-shirts from every team she'd been on, every softball camp she'd been to, every big tournament she'd played.

In this world KT had mostly plain T-shirts—red, blue, green, yellow, orange, and purple—and a smattering of T-shirts that said meaningless things like JOE'S COFFEE SHOP or I GO TO BRECKSVILLE NORTH. (If any writing-related ac team had been involved in coming up with that one, KT was pretty sure they were having a losing season.) This whole past week those shirts had made KT feel dull and dreary and deserving of no notice whatsoever. But at least today a couple of the colored ones would do as decent stand-ins for uniforms. She could loan some out if she needed to.

KT went downstairs to the kitchen and pulled out water bottles she'd stashed in both the refrigerator and the freezer overnight. Sure, it was cool outside right now, but if they played into the late afternoon, things might get a little steamy. She added the water bottles to the wagon in the garage, then tucked a twenty-dollar bill under the bottles. There were a few fast-food restaurants within walking distance of the park. Maybe everyone who showed up would want to go out for a late lunch afterward.

KT went back into the kitchen and forced herself to choke down a quick breakfast, even though she was almost too excited to eat. Dad was just stumbling into the kitchen as KT put her dishes in the sink. He had his head down, studying the Academics section of the newspaper.

"Guess what, Dad?" KT said. She hadn't mentioned her planned softball game to Mom or Dad all week long.

Superstitiously, she'd almost been afraid that if she told them, somehow this, too, would disappear from her world. Or Mom and Dad would take it away.

But she felt too hyped up to keep secrets any longer. It was finally Saturday. What could go wrong now?

And—wouldn't Dad want to come and watch?

"Hey, wasn't that a great game Max had last night?" Dad asked, barely bothering to glance up at KT.

"Yeah, but—," KT tried again.

Max appeared at the kitchen doorway, rubbing sleep out of his eyes. He yawned. Dad dropped the newspaper, grabbed Max around the shoulders, and gave him a noogie on the head. Then Dad faked a couple of punches at Max's chest.

"There's my boy!" Dad cheered. "My champion! What do you say the two of us hit the math books together today?"

Max darted his eyes quickly at KT, then back to Dad.

"Uh, maybe this afternoon?" Max said.

"What's wrong with right after breakfast?" Dad asked.

Max glanced at the clock on the microwave.

"Nothing, I guess," Max said.

Dad pulled out a chair at the kitchen table for Max.

"Here. Sit down. Want me to fix you pancakes? French toast? An omelet?" Dad asked Max. He looked over at KT as if he'd just remembered she was there. "KT, do you want any? Er, I guess you already ate, didn't you?" He glanced toward the dishes in the sink, then squinted at her a little blankly. "Oh. Were you saying something a minute ago?"

"Nothing, Dad," KT said. "Never mind."

She left the kitchen, trying to hold on to her excitement from a few moments ago.

Never mind is right, she told herself. *He wasn't interested enough for me to bother telling him anything. But it doesn't matter. All that matters is that I'm going to have softball again.*

This wasn't any different from a setback in a game. You just had to shake it off and keep going.

She decided to head to the park early.

"I'm leaving!" she called back to Dad and Max in the kitchen, even as she pushed the garage-door opener so she could pull out the wagon. "I'll probably be gone most of the day!"

She didn't wait to hear if Dad even bothered asking, "Where are you going?"

It took longer than she expected to roll the overloaded wagon all the way to the park. It was probably a good mile away, and KT's arms started hurting before she'd even gone halfway.

Oh, well. That will build better muscles for pitching, she told herself. *I probably haven't been getting enough practice this week, just pitching during that one short class every day at school.*

Soon enough the flat, open green of Ridgestone Park appeared before her. KT had picked this park because it was so huge—if enough people showed up to hold four games simultaneously, they could do that. Without backstops or fences everyone would just have to stay alert for runaway balls.

KT set out enough pillow bases for two diamonds, for a start. She stepped off the proper distances between bases and readjusted all of the pillows slightly. Somebody persnickety—Vanessa? Bree?—might bring a yardstick or something to measure it precisely, but KT was satisfied. She could feel the distances in her bones, could tell even with her eyes shut what it should feel like to run from base to base.

In the center of each diamond she stomped down the grass and dug in her cleats to mark the pitcher's place. She practiced the motion of each throw, whirling her arm just right without actually releasing any balls. Then she went to home base and practiced hitting tossed-up balls.

Probably some of the girls will be so eager they'll show up before ten, KT thought. *We can get started with an impromptu practice until everyone gets here.*

She reminded herself that she'd probably have to teach everyone the game, so she'd have to be patient and not expect them to play at a Rysdale Invitational level right away.

But they're all great athletes, she thought. *They'll learn fast.*

She targeted the location of all the balls she hit: *This one will go to second base,* she told herself. *This one will go to right field . . .*

She used up all the balls, then jogged out to collect them all. On her way back to home base, she stopped at the wagon to check the time on her phone: 9:56.

Any minute now, she told herself.

She kept batting, in between looking back toward the parking lot. *This one will go toward third base, but don't let it go foul,* she told herself. *Now, this one will go toward where a shortstop should be . . .*

She came to the bottom of the basket of balls once more. She was slow walking out to retrieve the balls again, slow walking over to the wagon, slow picking up her phone.

Ten fifteen.

She slid down to the ground, grabbed one of the water bottles, and gulped it down.

Maybe some of the girls got lost, she told herself, wiping the sweaty bottle against her own sweaty forehead. In one of her multiple mass messages, she'd given everyone her cell number—maybe she'd just missed hearing the phone. She checked both her missed-call log and the text-message in-box.

Nothing.

She watched the deserted parking lot.

Nothing.

At ten forty-five, she had to face the truth: Nobody had shown up. Nobody was going to.

Nobody.

KT pitched her head forward, burying her face in her hands. Then she collapsed all the way down to the ground. She wasn't much for crying, but she sobbed now; she wailed; she scared herself with how violently the tears came.

I can't get softball back, she thought. *I can't. No matter how hard I try, I can't play softball alone. I need a team and—nobody wants to be on a team with me.*

She pounded her fists on the ground, rubbed her face back and forth in the dirt.

Two hundred girls I contacted. Two hundred! All of them used to love softball. Most of them used to be my friends. And none of them even bothered writing back to say they weren't coming.

She was getting snot in her hair, mud in her ears.

How can I survive in this awful place without softball?
How can I ever get back to the real world now?

She felt a hand on her shoulder. She heard a voice.

"You were voted one of the best eighth-grade pitchers in the entire state. You pitched a no-hitter in that championship tournament game in Atlanta—or was it Houston? You'd think I'd remember, I've heard the story so many times."

KT lifted her head.

It wasn't one of her softball friends or teammates crouching beside her, holding her shoulder, trying to pull her up.

It was her brother, Max.

Chapter Eighteen

"You remember!" KT cried, springing up from the dirt. She wiped the mud and snot from her face onto her sleeve and grabbed her brother in a gigantic hug. "You remember the real world!"

"Won't . . . do you any good . . . if you squeeze me to death," Max struggled to say.

KT laughed. She let go for a minute, then hugged him again. She kept hugging him.

"I thought I was the only one who remembered," she babbled. "I thought I was going crazy!"

"This alternate world is crazy," Max agreed.

"Yeah, it's even worse than something out of one of your video ga—" KT stopped herself. She pulled back from hugging Max. "Wait a minute—you did this, didn't you? You zapped us into some sort of video game!" She began hitting Max, slapping him on the arm, punching him in the shoulder. The hits got harder and harder. "Get me out of here!"

Max shoved her away.

"If I was creating some sort of alternate world to make myself happy, do you think I'd make it so I spend five hours every school day exercising?" he snarled. "Do you think I'd make it so I have Mom and Dad breathing down my neck every minute at home, Coach Horace breathing down my neck every spare minute at school—'Practice your math! Make sure your grades are high enough to play! Practice your math some more!'? Do you think I like this world any more than you do?"

KT stared at her brother. He had a streak of mud across his cheek—mud that had smeared from her face onto his. He didn't bother rubbing it off. He was still lazy. And he was still pudgy and pasty and everything else that had always disgusted and annoyed her about Max.

But he was the real Max, the one she'd known his entire life. He was exactly who he'd always been. She didn't have to go guessing about how he'd become a different person, growing up in this different world.

She knew him. And . . . she believed him.

"No," she whispered. "No, I don't think this is the alternate world you'd make, if you could make things the way you wanted." She tilted her head thoughtfully. "So—did you just make some sort of mistake? Can you fix it and send me back?"

"KT, I'm not the one who set up this horrible world!" Max protested. "I don't know any more than you do about why it exists or how we got here!"

"Oh," KT said. She sagged against the side of the red wagon. "But . . . we're a team now. We both want the same thing. We can work together figuring out how to get out of here."

It was weird how much better this made her feel. This was

just her no-good slug of a brother, Max. And he'd already said he didn't know anything.

But he remembered the real world, and the real KT. And he didn't hate her so much that he wasn't willing to help get all of that back.

"Okay," Max said evenly. He scooted over and leaned back against the wagon, sitting right beside her. "Where do you think we should start? What have you figured out so far?"

"Not much," KT said. She shrugged. "The last thing I remember from the real world was during a softball game—the fifth inning of the Rysdale championship game. So I thought, if I could just play a softball game here, it could be like, like . . ."

"The doorway back?" Max asked skeptically.

Spoken out loud, the idea sounded ludicrous. KT wrinkled her nose.

"Maybe I just really, really, really wanted to play softball," she admitted, looking sadly out at the empty pillow bases spread across the grass. "I *wanted* that to be an answer."

"When you're a hammer, all you see is nails," Max muttered.

"Huh?" KT said.

"It's a saying. All you ever think about is softball, so of course you wanted that to be the answer," Max said.

He said this almost fondly, so somehow it didn't make KT mad.

"Yeah, well, what's the last thing you remember about the real world?" KT asked. "What was your 'doorway'?"

"I don't know," Max admitted. "The last thing I remember was at your game, too—"

"The Rysdale championship?"

"I guess," he said. "On Sunday. I was playing Starship

Defense on my DS. And then I must have blacked out, because the next thing I remember it was Monday morning and Mom was waking me up telling me it was my big day. And I didn't have a clue what she was talking about."

"Because you were in weirdo world," KT finished for him. "I heard Mom say that too."

She stared off into the cloudless sky—like the cloudless skies she'd seen over countless softball fields in the real world, but completely and utterly different because this whole world was different.

She'd never thought of cloudless skies as empty before.

She looked back, and Max was just watching her stare off into space.

"So we both blacked out right before things changed," she said briskly, trying to bring herself back to KT-gets-things-done mode. "Do you remember any pain? Did anything hurt when you blacked out?"

Max squinted, thinking.

"Maybe," he said slowly. "It's hard to remember. . . . Do you think the same thing zapped us both, at exactly the same time?"

"I don't know," KT said. "For me, the last thing I remember is throwing the ball to make the third out in the fifth inning. Did you blank out at the top of the fifth, too?"

"How should I know?" Max asked. "I wasn't paying attention to your game! I was fighting aliens!"

Back in the real world it would have made KT furious that he'd been at her softball game and not even watched. He'd just been fighting some stupid imaginary war.

But she'd been at his mathletics game last night and not watched either. She'd just sat there longing for softball.

"Mom and Dad made you go to my game, didn't they?" KT asked. She snorted. "Let me guess—they said, 'You have to be supportive of your sister. In this family we support the important efforts of each individual member.' Right?"

"That and, 'This is what being a family is all about,'" Max quoted, in such a great imitation of Mom's voice that KT laughed. "And, 'Max, we want to spend time with both our kids. If you don't come to the game, we'll barely see you today.'"

At least KT hadn't been given that excuse. Maybe she should be insulted that this world's Mom didn't want to spend time with her.

Max dug his heel into the grass.

"Mom and I got into a huge fight that day, right before we got in the car," he said. "I told her, 'Yeah, well, why don't you make KT watch me play video games?'"

"Max, that'd be awful," KT protested. "I'd hate it!"

"I wasn't *serious*," Max said. "I wouldn't want you guys watching me either." He twisted up his face in disgust. "I was just trying to make a point. Why were your games so important, and all anybody ever talked about, when the games I played always had Mom yelling at me, 'Max, shut that thing off! Go do something useful!'?"

"Because—," KT began, ready to hotly defend the honor of softball versus video games.

Max held up his hands, stopping her.

"I know! I know!" he said. "Believe me, Mom told me every single reason. 'Because what KT does is healthy. It's exercise. It's hard work. It's *achievement*. It could get her a college scholarship. It could lead to international fame and a high-profile coaching job or TV commentator job, and a lifetime of signing autographs for people who run into her at the mall.' Or something like that."

Back in the real world that would have been the cue for KT to screech, "Don't joke about my future like that! Mom's *right*! Softball is a billion times more important than video games!"

But KT had been dealing with Nasty Mom all week. She knew what it felt like to have her mother's every look and every word carry the secret or not-so-secret background message: *I'm not interested in what you're interested in. I'm not really even that interested in you.*

"I guess . . . I guess some video games are exercise," KT said. "Like, Wii or Kinect. And . . . if it's all about preparing for the future . . . people do get jobs making video games. They talked about that at Career Day at school. Some computer programmers make a lot of money."

Max gaped at her.

"You—you're defending me?" he asked incredulously.

"When we get back to the real world, I'll tell Mom and Dad to lay off your case about the video games," KT said. "And I'll tell them not to make you go to my softball games if you don't want to."

Max just kept staring. KT felt a little bit like she always felt in the pitching circle: powerful. In control. Maybe like a queen dispensing favors.

"Thank you," Max whispered.

KT remembered she wasn't powerful or in control in this world. She was nobody and nothing at home, and everybody hated her at school. And not a single one of her former friends from the real world had shown up to play softball.

"Yeah, well, that's when we get back to the real world," KT

said. *"You're* the one who has the pull with Mom and Dad here."

"I'll tell them not to make you go to my mathletics games, then," Max said.

"Why don't we just get out of here before there's another mathletics game?" KT asked.

"I have mathletics club-team tryouts tomorrow," Max said glumly. "Seven hours of people watching me do math, evaluating my every move."

KT watched Max, her head cocked.

"Max," she said slowly. "Forget the part about having everybody watch you—do you even like math? Were you that good at it in the real world?"

KT tried to remember if she'd ever heard Mom or Dad talking about Max's math brilliance in the real world. Mom had told Mrs. Bashkov about KT's good grades in this world—surely if Max had been some math genius for real, there would have been some moment when Mom or Dad would have said, "Way to go, Max! I can't believe you had the highest math grade in your whole class!" They would have come back from parent-teacher conferences saying, "Wow, Max, your teacher says your mind is made for math!" or whatever that ridiculous thing was that Mom had quoted in this world. They wouldn't have been nearly as excited about it as they were here, and Dad probably would have gone right back to talking about sports, but still. Why couldn't KT remember anything like that?

KT kept racking her brain, but came up blank. Max was frowning.

"I never thought math was hard," he said. "Sometimes it was kind of fun. But mostly I just got in trouble in math and always had points taken off because I wouldn't show my work."

KT rolled her eyes.

"Good old lazy Max," she muttered.

"No," Max said, but it wasn't like he was being defensive. It was more like he was figuring something out. "I don't think I was being lazy. Really. It was more like—there wasn't any work to show. I just looked at the problems and I knew the answer. If they forced me to write something down, to show my steps, I always had to make something up."

KT remembered how he'd seemed to know the answers instantly during the mathletics game yesterday, the parts she'd actually paid attention to.

She slugged him in the arm.

"Whoa, Max," she said. "You really are a math genius!"

"Well," he said modestly, "I don't think it will work that way when I get to the harder stuff—calculus, trigonometry, all that. Ben says his parents say the American school system really doesn't expect enough of sixth graders in math. That's why they had him pushed up to seventh-grade math, in the real world. He wanted me to take the test to see if I could do that too, but, you know, everyone at school already thought I was a nerd. I didn't need to make it worse."

KT felt a little pang in her heart. She'd always kind of thought that Max didn't know how uncool he was. He was like some big, sloppy, happy dog lolling through life, not even hearing the complaints: "Yuck! He drools!" "He smells!" "He just made a mess!"

Not that I think Max drools, but . . . but didn't he think people liked him? KT thought. *Wasn't he happy?*

Somehow these weren't questions she could ask her brother.

Instead she put on a show of total outrage. She put her hands on her hips.

"Maxwell Charles Sutton!" she said. "Are you telling me you had the chance to hit the ball out of the ballpark, and you didn't even bother stepping up to the plate to bat?"

"It wasn't *softball*," Max said defiantly. "And I'm not *you*. I don't need people telling me how great I am all the time. I don't need to show off!"

KT remembered the hissed comments she'd heard at school: *Show-off!* Was that true? Was she just a show-off?

Nobody criticized me for trying to do my best on the softball field, she thought. *At Max's mathletics game yesterday, nobody criticized Max for getting the answers before everyone else. They cheered!*

KT dropped her arms.

"I'm just kidding," she said, though she kind of wasn't. She squinted, trying to recapture the trail of a thought she'd been working on before. "What I don't get is, it's kind of like you and me switched places coming to this world, right?"

"Yeah, I guess," Max said.

"But in the real world, you liked video games and I liked softball," KT said. "So why didn't video games and sports switch? How'd all the school stuff get involved? Why didn't it become video-game tournaments that Mom and Dad care about so much, video games that you have club teams for, video games that you practice constantly after school?"

"Now, that would be *sweet*," Max said. He grinned. Then the grin faded. "But you're right . . ." A troubled look came over his face. He reached back into the wagon and pulled out two of the softballs, one that was a grayish white and one that was a battered pink. He put them both on the ground in front of him, pointing to first one and then the other, muttering, "Real-world Max forced to go to KT's games. Alt-world KT forced to go to Max's."

He kept switching the balls back and forth, muttering about the differences between the two worlds. KT heard, ". . . football players are the coolest kids in sixth grade; Ben Bashkov is the coolest kid in sixth grade. . . . Mom and Dad want Max to do sports; Mom and Dad want KT to do acs. . . ."

KT realized she was watching Max do the equivalent of finally showing his work. He was trying to figure out a solution that was harder than sixth-grade math.

He reached back into the wagon and pulled out an icy water bottle. He put it an equal distance from each of the two softballs. Then he began switching all three items around, muttering, "Sports . . . school . . . video games . . . KT . . . Max . . . and . . ."

He stopped with the water bottle and the two softballs in a triangular formation on the ground.

"Here's the answer," Max announced.

"What?" KT asked.

"It's not just you and me who got flipped around," Max said. "There's someone else involved. Someone else whose problems got mixed up with ours, who cares a lot more about school than either of us do. Because there's that extra variable. And that other person probably remembers the real world too."

"So, you think," KT began, "to get back to the real world . . ."

Max pointed at the sweaty water bottle tilting in the grass.

"We've got to find that third person," he said.

Chapter Nineteen

"So who is it?" KT asked.

"How should I know?" Max asked. "I thought I was doing pretty well, figuring out this much."

He waved his hand toward the softballs and the water bottle.

"How do you know it's not, like, two other people? Or more? Like . . . a whole softball team?" KT asked hopefully.

"Occam's razor," Max said.

"Huh?" KT asked.

"It's a scientific principle," Max said. "Try the simplest explanation first. Having it be just one more person is easiest, so that's the possibility we should consider—and rule out, if we have to—before thinking about anything else."

"How do you *know* stuff like that?" KT asked. "Oscar's razor—"

"Occam's," Max corrected.

"And that thing about the hammer and the nails—"

"Hey, I've been hanging out with Ben Bashkov since I was five," Max said. "He thinks you need to haul out scientific principles and philosophical debate just to decide how to eat an Oreo."

KT rolled her eyes. Then she caught herself.

"Wait—what if Ben is the third person?" she said. "That's got to be it! He's really smart. He gets good grades. People think he's a nerd in the real world, but he's cool here. This world is *made* for Ben Bashkov! Er—I'm sorry—'Ebenezer.' Right? Aren't I right?"

Max shook his head.

"No," he said. "The real Ben is a nice guy. In this world he's a total jerk. He's stringing along four different girls who all think he's their boyfriend, and he loves it that they're all jealous of one another."

It's people like that who give jocks a bad image, KT thought. *I mean . . . mathletes.*

She bit her lip.

"Well, no offense," she began. "But what if that's what Ben really wants to be like in the real world, but he's not cool enough to have any girl like him, let alone *four*? What if this world is just bringing out his real personality?"

"No," Max said stubbornly, shaking his head even harder. "That's not Ben. Anyhow, even if he wanted to be like that, the real Ben couldn't do it. Ever since we started sixth grade, he's been terrified of talking to *any* girl. He couldn't just switch that off. He's not the real Ben here."

KT had kind of forgotten how freaky sixth-grade boys could be. She pictured the goofy, awkward, gangly Ben she knew in the real world, and put that image beside the obnoxious, overconfident kid she'd seen at the mathletics game last night.

Max was right. The bony knees might be the same, but it wasn't the same kid.

"What about your other friends?" KT said. "Do you think it could be any of them?"

"Um," Max said, suddenly acting incredibly interested in the beads of water dripping down the bottle. "I don't actually have any other friends besides Ben. Not in the real world."

He seemed to be trying very hard to act like that was no big deal, like he was just making an ordinary statement: "The sky is blue." "The grass is green." "I don't have any other friends." But KT felt another deep pang. She wanted to go beat up all those stupid sixth graders who wouldn't be friends with Max: *What's wrong with you? Huh? Huh? Don't you know you're missing out, not being friends with my brother?*

Even though, back in the real world, she hadn't exactly paid attention to him either.

She didn't say anything.

"I don't really think I have any friends in this world either," Max said, very carefully. "Not real ones. I don't think people count as friends if they're just hanging around me because I'm a mathlete and that makes them look popular."

"You're right," KT said fiercely. "Fake friends don't count! Better one *real* friend than a million, uh . . ."

Max shrugged helplessly, and KT had to say *something*.

"Well, you see all my friends in this world," she said, gesturing at the empty softball diamond. "Two hundred girls just made it very clear that they aren't my friends here. I don't even have a Ben!"

She'd meant to sound too sarcastic to let any pain through,

but her throat caught a little, closing over the words *"aren't my friends"* . . .

"KT—," Max began.

"And I know none of them are the mysterious third person we're looking for, because I put these, like, codes in my messages about this softball game, referring to things in the real world," KT said. "And no one picked up on them. No one. No one even asked, 'What are you talking about?'"

"Well, that's—," Max tried again.

KT grabbed Max's arm.

"Wait—do you think that means none of them actually got my messages?" KT asked excitedly. "I was sending out eight or ten messages a day some days, and nobody answered any of them after that first day. Of course! It all makes sense now! I just need to figure out how to fix my Facebook account, and then—"

"KT," Max interrupted. "Listen to yourself. You were sending out eight or ten messages a day to total strangers. Yeah, you think of them as friends, but they don't remember you. People didn't answer because . . . because . . ." He swallowed hard, and then almost whispered, "You sounded like a crazy stalker."

Now Max sounded embarrassed on her behalf.

KT felt her face go red. Was Max right? She tried to imagine getting eight or ten messages a day from a total stranger in the real world.

Yeah, crazy stalker, she thought. *That's what I'd think.*

Her face flamed even more. Suddenly it seemed as hard to catch her breath as it had been that time a softball slammed into her gut. She could just picture two hundred girls at once deleting her messages, blocking her new messages, hitting ignore in response to her Facebook friend requests. She could even imagine some of them copying her messages over and forwarding them to their actual friends with sarcastic comments: *Can you believe what this whack job's been sending me?* Vanessa would do that. Maybe Molly, too. And . . .

"I'm sorry," Max muttered. "If it makes you feel any better, those messages wouldn't have seemed weird to anybody who knew you. It's just . . ."

It's just you're the only one who knows the real me in this world, KT thought, aching all over again. *You and maybe some mystery person who definitely isn't one of my friends.*

But she'd kept sending out those messages, kept telling herself the softball game was going to happen, no matter what. Because that was the kind of thing she did in the real world. No matter how high the odds were stacked against you, no matter how much evidence there was that you were going to lose, you still tried and tried and tried; you played your guts out; you *believed* you were going to win. And, in KT's experience, usually you did. Working hard and believing in yourself could win out over odds and evidence.

But now she was almost hoping that her former friends had just deleted the messages without reading them, or had blocked her messages completely. Except . . .

"Wait a minute," she said, looking back at Max. "How do *you* know what my messages sounded like? Did you read them?"

"Um . . . ," Max said, looking uncomfortable again. Then he gulped once more and said, almost defiantly, "How do you think I knew to look for you here?"

KT hadn't even thought to wonder about that.

"You hacked into my Facebook account?" she asked incredulously.

"I didn't pull any pranks on you or anything, honest!" Max said. "I just had to know . . . I kind of thought Monday night that you were the real you, and you remembered the real world. Because you called Dad out, and told him he was an accountant, not someone doing hard physical labor every day."

"Hold on," KT said, actually putting her hands up like a traffic cop. "You're telling me that you've known since *Monday* that you and I are on the same team, and that neither one of us has to be alone in all this, and you waited until now— Saturday, *five days later*—to tell me?"

"I didn't know Monday that we were on the same team," Max said softly. "I was pretty sure you remembered the real world, but . . . how was I supposed to know that would make us teammates? You still acted like you hated me."

It was funny—Max hadn't been on a single sports team since kindergarten, and he could still nail KT on the definition of "team."

"I never *hated* you," KT said defensively. "I was just avoiding you because I promised Mom I wouldn't say anything bad to you about mathletics. And I didn't want to think about anything but softball."

"Just like in the real world," Max muttered.

KT felt oddly ashamed.

"I didn't hate you there, either," KT said. "I just . . . get annoyed. You're my kid brother and . . ." And when was the last time in the real world that she'd looked at him with anything but contempt and disgust? Loathing, even?

There was nothing else she could say except, "I'm sorry."

Max shrugged.

"It doesn't matter now," he said.

KT couldn't tell if he was forgiving her or not.

"Hey," she said. "How'd you know how to hack into Facebook, anyhow? Are you secretly a computer genius too?"

"All I had to do was figure out your password," he said.

"Yeah, I guess 'Olympics2024' is pretty obvious," KT said.

"No, your password in this world is 'StraightAs,'" Max said. He made a face, scrunching up his nose. "Real original of you. That's Ben's password in the real world."

KT stared at Max in dismay. She always left herself logged in to Facebook—it saved time she'd rather use on softball. *Or, it'd be time for schoolwork, here in this world,* she thought, grimacing. Either way, she hadn't seen the different password.

"You mean to tell me there was some weirdo-world version of me making up stupid passwords like that before I woke up here Monday morning?" KT asked. "Is that how this works?"

"I guess," Max said, though he looked dubious. "There had to have been some version of both of us here before, or else Mom and Dad would have screamed when we showed up in their house. Everyone at school would have looked at us like we were strangers. Someone named KT Sutton and someone named Max Sutton were here before we arrived."

"So did we all just trade places?" KT asked. "Is there a weirdo-world me—and a weirdo-world you—running around in the real world?"

"That's one possible scenario," Max said.

Weirdo-world KT better not have messed up the end of the Rysdale Invitational, KT thought.

She felt a little bit like she had the first time she'd played in a softball league where players were allowed to steal bases.

Suddenly pitching wasn't just about making great throws; it was also about seeing everything around her at once, knowing who was thinking of running when—and knowing how to stop them.

"I know, I know—thinking about that is like going from playing a 2-D video game to a 3-D one," Max said.

Why do you have to compare everything to a video game? KT wanted to ask. But then what would she say if he asked, *Why do you have to compare everything to softball?*

Something was bugging her, tickling the back of her mind. It was like having a runner behind her on second who was acting all sweet-as-pie and *What? Me? You think I'd actually try to steal third?* When KT knew she couldn't trust the runner for an instant. Some detail didn't seem right . . .

Suddenly KT remembered what it was.

"Oh, Max," she said. "Max, Max, Max. I think I just figured this out! I know who the third person is!"

"Who?" Max said.

"I think, I think . . ." KT hadn't actually worked out all the details. She was still putting things together. "It's Dad."

Max did a double take.

"Mr. 'I Live for Math'?" he asked. "I don't get it."

"No, no, it makes sense," KT said. "He's an accountant in the real world, right? So he actually is good at math. And he likes it. Or—I guess he does." She'd never actually thought to wonder whether her dad liked his job. She'd certainly never asked him. "I don't know why he hasn't admitted the truth to us yet. Maybe he's trying to teach us a lesson or something. But here's my proof. Have you tried opening our garage door since Monday? Even if my Facebook password changed, the code for our garage door is still 2024—the year I'm going to the Olympics. Dad's the one who programmed that, so he still remembers the real world. He's got to!"

It would be great having Dad on their team. She kind of felt like a little girl again, knowing Daddy would take care of her.

He'll get us back to the real world, KT thought. *He wants me to get that University of Arizona scholarship and play in the Olympics as much as I do!*

But Max was shaking his head.

"I'm sorry," he said. "The garage code is 2024 in this world because that's when Mom and Dad think I'm going to play in the International Mathlympics. Dad only mentioned it seven times this morning when he was helping me practice math."

"Oh," KT said. She slumped over, as deflated as a balloon that had lost all its air.

"But you're on the right track," Max said, and this was even more demoralizing, that he was trying so hard to cheer her up. "I think we should be looking for things that are a little off, details that are out of place in this world—hints that some-body brought some piece of the real world with them. Like you trying to set up a softball tournament or talking about Dad being an accountant, and me—"

"What did you do?" KT asked curiously. "Did something happen that I should have noticed?"

"Well, I was terrible at mathletics on Monday," Max said. "I froze up completely because—do you know how much pres-sure even a middle-school mathlete is under?"

"Try being a middle-school pitcher," KT muttered.

"How do you stand it?" Max asked, and it seemed like he really wanted to know.

"I like it," KT said. This was and wasn't true, all at once. "It makes me play better. Because . . . it makes me feel important."

Max was shaking his head.

"You're crazy," he said. "It just made me want to throw up."

KT laughed.

"But you played pretty well yesterday," she said.

"Yeah, because I'd decided this whole world was fake, and nothing I did here mattered," Max said.

"Do you still think that?" KT asked. "Do you think we could rob banks or—I don't know, kill people—and it wouldn't be any big deal?"

"I think we probably shouldn't test out anything that extreme until we're sure," Max said.

KT laughed again. She was actually enjoying hanging out with Max. That was maybe the weirdest part of this weird world.

"You want to know the worst thing I did, when I first got to this world?" Max said. "On Monday I was so bad at running on the treadmill that I actually shot out the back. Flew halfway across the room and slammed into the wall. It was like something out of a cartoon!"

"Did you get in trouble?" KT asked.

"No, Ben told the teacher I was just nervous about the mathletics game, and she let me set my treadmill on a really slow speed," Max said. He looked a little wistful. "It is kind of nice having the teachers give me special treatment. Because I'm a jock now—er, a Spock."

"A Spock?" KT asked.

"You know, that's what they call kids in this world who do mathletics or chemademics or some other ac," Max said. "I'm guessing it's from that old TV show *Star Trek*—wasn't Mr. Spock the really smart guy?"

KT realized that Max must have been paying more attention to the oddities of this world than she had.

"Wouldn't you think it'd be the kids who are good at school who get the special treatment from teachers?" KT complained. "I had Mr. Horace yelling at me and Mr. Huck acting all weird about some e-mail I supposedly sent—it must have been something weird-world KT did before I got here, right?"

Max squinted at KT.

"What did the e-mail say?" he asked.

"I don't know. I never checked," KT said. "I was too busy planning for this softball tournament." She gestured toward the empty bases once more, but her brain was already moving past that. "Wait a minute, this really doesn't make sense, does it? Mr. Horace is like the football coach in the real world, and the football coach wouldn't go out of his way to yell at some random kid who gets straight As. And some of the stuff Mr. Huck said, about how the school has its priorities messed up, and it's students like me who get hurt . . ."

She reached back into the wagon and pulled out her iPod.

"Let's see if I can get Wi-Fi out here, to look it up," she said, scrolling through her choices.

"You think Mr. Huck or Mr. Horace remembers the real world?" Max asked. "You think one of them is our mystery person?"

"One of them, or . . ." KT got distracted logging on to the Internet. She quickly clicked into her e-mail account, and scrolled back through her sent file. Why would she—or rather weird-world KT—have bothered with e-mail instead of just sending a Facebook message?

"This must be it," KT said. "This e-mail went out a week

ago Friday to Mr. Arnold, Mrs. Szymanski, Mr. Horace, and all these other teachers—er, coaches?"

Max was looking over her shoulder.

"So you hit the principal, the vice principal, the academic director, and it looks like coaches and assistant coaches for every single ac," he muttered. "What did you say to all of them?"

KT scrolled down to the text of the e-mail:

To the administration, teachers, and coaches of Brecksville Middle School North:

All my life I have been told that the point of school is to prepare students for adulthood and the world of work. The way everyone acts at our school, you would think that all of us are going to grow up to do professional acs. Oh, sure, the teachers make a halfhearted effort to teach us running, throwing, biking and lifting—the skills 99.9 percent of us will actually need in our adult lives. But very few teachers try to challenge us to work to our fullest potential. If a student on her own works really, really hard in class, other students—and sometimes even the teachers themselves—make fun of her.

Instead, the students who consistently get held up as role models and praised and rewarded the most for their efforts are the ones who do acs. The greatest energy and enthusiasm in this school always goes toward mathletics, chemademics, etc. Why do we waste valuable classroom time going to pep rallies for acs? Why are the morning announcements always about which team won which game the night before? Why is the first thing anyone sees walking into the school the trophy case of academic trophies? Why does Principal Arnold on the first day of school each year tell all the sixth graders that the best way to take full advantage of a Brecksville North education is to be an athlete-scholar and make sure that they get involved in acs?

I have a great idea. Why don't we cancel all the acs, and have the teachers and coaches use all the energy they usually put into acs for making classes as fun and interesting and educational as possible? And for making students the best *students* they can be? Why don't we make school important as school, not just as an excuse to play acs?

Sincerely,
KT Sutton

KT blinked.

"Ninety-nine-point-nine percent of kids will need to do exercises on their jobs in this world?" she asked. "It's not just Mom and Dad running on treadmills?"

Max was reading the e-mail over her shoulder.

"It's almost like you have to translate this," he said. "Substitute the word 'sports' for 'acs' everywhere, and that's kind of how things were in the real world."

"The school never put too much emphasis on sports!" KT protested.

"It felt that way for people who weren't any good at sports," Max muttered.

KT wanted to keep protesting, but Max was already moving on to another point.

"Do you think somebody sent an e-mail like this one—or the reverse of this one—in the real world?" he asked. "Someone who's as crazy about math or chemistry or some other academic subject as you are about softball?"

KT's eyes blurred staring at the e-mail.

"Yeah," she said slowly. "Yeah, I'm sure of it."

"You're *sure?*" Max asked doubtfully.

"Last week," KT said. "All the spring athletes got called down to the gym for a special meeting." She put the words "special meeting" in air quotes. "None of us knew what it was about, but Mr. Neal, the athletic director, went on and on about how we of all people were supposed to be role models, and we must never, ever bully anybody who wasn't as athletically gifted as we were. . . . We all just thought it was stupid, and that's why I forgot about it until now."

"But you think that lecture was because someone sent an e-mail like this," Max finished for her.

"And I know who it was," KT said.

Someone who's as crazy about math or chemistry or some other academic subject as you are about softball, Max had said. And KT herself had sat through the mathletics competition the day before, watching the star player—the team's pitcher, as it were—and thought she was as fierce and feisty at math as KT was at softball. This girl had literally taken KT's place in the cafeteria, taking KT's seat with Molly and Lex.

"You're thinking of Evangeline, aren't you?" Max asked.

Chapter Twenty

KT picked up the two softballs and the sweating water bottle and tossed them back into the wagon. She stood up and lifted the wagon's handle.

"Wait—what are you doing?" Max asked.

"We're going to go find Evangeline," KT said, giving the handle a tug to pull it toward the first pillow "base." "Do you know where she lives?"

"No, but—are you sure—"

KT tossed him the iPod.

"You look up her address and I'll pick up all the pillows. Hurry," KT said.

She jogged around the two makeshift softball diamonds, grabbing up the pillows as quickly as she could.

When she got back to Max, he had his cell phone up to his ear.

"You're calling her?" KT asked, horrified. She swiped her hand at his cell phone and punched the button to hang up.

"Don't do that! Don't give her any warning that we're coming! We need every advantage we can get! She's . . . well, you know, she's a lot smarter than us!"

"I wasn't calling Evangeline," Max protested. "I was calling home to get Mom or Dad to drive us over there. Evangeline lives on Apple Valley Drive—it's a million miles away!"

"Let me see that," KT said, pulling the iPod out of Max's other hand. She squinted at the map he'd called up. "You're crazy! It's just ten or eleven blocks. We get Mom and Dad involved in this, they'll want to know why we're going to Evangeline's—you can use math as an excuse, but they know *I'd* never have anything to do with her!"

Max didn't argue, but he frowned as he stood up stiffly. KT jerked the wagon forward, then glanced back to make sure Max was following her. He was just now taking his first step, awkward and limping.

"What's wrong with you?" KT asked. "Leg cramp up or something?"

"Sort of," Max muttered.

He winced as he took his next step too. He was shuffling along like some hundred-year-old arthritic great-grandfather. It hurt just to watch.

"Really, are you okay?" KT asked.

"Of course I'm not okay!" Max exploded. "Every muscle in my body is in agony! Muscles I didn't even know I had before are screaming out, 'Don't take another step! The pain'll kill you!'"

All that exercise, KT thought. *Five or six hours a day, every day last week at school. After years of Max doing nothing but sitting in front of a computer or video game screen, being a blob. Of course he's in pain.*

"Don't say it!" Max warned, taking another halting step forward. "Don't say, 'Geez, Max, if only you were a finely tuned athlete like me, you could run to Evangeline's house at top speed and not even start breathing hard!' Don't say, 'This is what you get for being fat!'"

He actually had tears glistening in his eyes. But the part of KT's brain that automatically would have labeled him a pathetic loser had switched off somehow.

"Poor Max," she said.

Max looked at her skeptically, as if he thought she was being sarcastic.

"Really," KT said. "Suddenly starting to exercise five or six hours a day is the totally wrong way to get into a fitness regime. You're lucky you didn't do any serious damage."

"How do you know I didn't?" Max muttered.

"You *can* still walk, can't you?" KT asked. "And—it gets a little better with every step, right?"

"I guess," Max said, sounding a little surprised as he took the next step.

"So, see, walking it off is the best thing you can do," KT said. And then, just in case he thought she was being smug rather than sincere, she added, "And anyhow, just think if we'd been zapped into a world where we had to do video games five or six hours a day. I'm sure I'd be in agony with serious, uh, thumb strain."

Max laughed.

"Thumb strain," he repeated, rolling his eyes.

And somehow, the way he said it was so hilarious that KT started laughing too. They lurched forward, KT pulling the wagon, Max limping unsteadily, both of them pitching side to side with gales of laughter.

This is fun, KT thought in amazement. And even though KT had actually wanted to rush to Evangeline's as quickly as possible—and get out of weirdo world as quickly as possible and get back to her beloved softball as quickly as possible— she found that she could slow down to Max's pace without any problem at all.

It was almost noon when they rounded the corner and turned onto Apple Valley Drive. Max squinted down the street.

"I can't make out the house number yet, but I bet I know which one is Evangeline's," Max said.

"The purple one?" KT asked.

In the row of ordinary brown and gray and tan and white houses, the eggplant-colored one with the fuchsia trim might as well have had a sign out front proclaiming, WEIRDEST KID IN SCHOOL LIVES HERE. Actually, as KT and Max walked closer, she realized there *were* signs out front, lined up above the garage: BRECKSVILLE MIDDLE SCHOOL NORTH CHEMADEMICS CHAMPION LIVES HERE and BRECKSVILLE MIDDLE SCHOOL NORTH MATHLETICS CHAMPION LIVES HERE and BRECKSVILLE MIDDLE SCHOOL NORTH POETRY SLAM CHAMPION LIVES HERE.

"She's a three-sport athlete?" Max muttered. "I mean—a three-ac Spock? I didn't know she did poetry slam too."

"Of course the PTO sells ac signs instead of athletic signs in this messed-up world," KT muttered back. "Of course."

She blinked hard, remembering a rare argument she'd had with her parents in the real world. They'd wanted so badly to buy one of the Brecksville North softball signs, but KT had thrown a fit, complaining, "No, I am *not* bragging about being on a middle-school team! Not when they let girls make it through tryouts who've never even played before!"

Maybe I sounded a little bit bratty, she thought now. *If I ever get back to the real world, maybe I will let Mom and Dad get the stupid sign, just to make them happy.*

When, I mean. When I get back to the real world . . .

"So why don't Mom and Dad have a mathletics sign nailed to our garage at home?" Max asked.

"You're a sixth grader," KT said distractedly. "This is your first year. You earn the sign this season, and then you'll have it."

She wondered why she hadn't noticed any of the ac signs in her own neighborhood that very first day when she was jogging to school.

I wasn't paying attention, she thought. *I wasn't thinking about anything but finding out about the Rysdale Invitational. And then, every day since then, I've just been thinking about setting up my softball league.*

She forced herself to look past the ac signs in Evangeline's yard. Wind chimes were lined up along the top of the front porch. Canning jars full of flowers leaned precariously around the base of every tree. Odd holes sprouted up at intervals across the grass, filled with what seemed to be carefully stacked pine cones.

Is that supposed to be some kind of landscaping art? KT wondered. *Or—a science experiment?*

KT glanced around at the nearby houses, all so boring and predictable.

Yeah, Evangeline's house is the weirdest in the neighborhood, KT thought. *But . . . it's also the most interesting.*

"Um, KT?" Max said. "Don't you think we might look kind of like stalkers, just standing here staring at Evangeline's house?"

"Oh, right," KT said. She walked over to the nearest drive-way and pulled her wagonful of softball supplies out into the street, ready to cross over toward Evangeline's.

"And maybe you should hide that wagon somewhere," Max suggested, trailing behind her. "Just so you don't look too . . . too . . ."

"Strange?" KT asked. "Is that what you're trying to say? Because it'd be strange in this world to be seen with anything related to sports?"

"Um . . . ," Max began.

KT gave an extra-hard tug on the wagon handle.

"Well, for your information, I thought we could *use* this to flush out Evangeline, if she doesn't want to help us," KT said, even though she'd thought no such thing until now.

"You're going to beat Evangeline with a softball bat to get her to tell you what you want to know?" Max asked, sounding horrified.

"*No*," KT protested. "I'm going to let her see the softball supplies and see if she acts like she recognizes them."

"Oh," Max said.

He didn't try again to suggest hiding the wagon, even though there was a bush right at the edge of Evangeline's yard that would have been perfect for that. But their easy camaraderie had disappeared.

"Go ring the doorbell," KT instructed.

Max hesitated at the bottom of the porch steps.

"Do you actually have a plan, or are we just going to wing it?" he asked.

"Look, you just get Evangeline to come out on the porch and talk to us," KT said. "I'll do the rest."

She didn't have a plan. She remembered what she'd told Max before, that Evangeline was smarter than both of them. She dropped the handle of her wagon so she could wipe sweat from her palms. She tried to ignore the nervous churning in her stomach.

Just think of this as pitching, she told herself. *You're going to pitch questions at Evangeline. And, yeah, she's smarter than you, but at the Rysdale Invitational Chelisha was a better softball player than you and you still got two strikes on her. And then . . .*

It didn't help to think about how great KT had been at the Rysdale Invitational when she didn't know how the game had ended.

Max was standing right in front of Evangeline's door now. He reached one trembling finger up to press the doorbell—which KT saw now was in the open mouth of a grinning gargoyle. From the inside of the house KT heard a sudden torrent of some kind of bizarre, atonal music.

Okay, so I guess Evangeline's family personalized their doorbell sounds the way other people personalize their cellphone ring tones, KT thought.

Max looked nervously back at KT. KT nodded reassuringly and stepped a little closer.

The heavy wood door creaked open behind the screen door. KT saw Evangeline's elfin features through the screen.

"Maxwell!" she cried, her face lighting up. "Did you come over to work together on math prep for tomorrow?"

Okay, this is going to be easy, KT thought. *Does little Evangeline maybe have a little crush on my brother?*

KT saw that Evangeline was reaching for the handle of the

screen door, either to push her way out to Max or to invite him in. But then Evangeline's hand froze.

"You brought your sister?" Evangeline asked.

Maybe KT should have hidden herself *and* the wagon. But it was too late now to activate that plan. Max was gazing speechlessly back and forth between Evangeline and KT. KT decided the best thing to do was just step up behind him.

"We just wanted to talk to you," KT said, as soothingly as she could. "Both of us did."

Evangeline let her hand drop to her side, leaving the screen door still firmly latched between her and the two Suttons.

"What about?" she asked guardedly.

Just be glad she didn't shut the wood door too, KT told herself. *She's willing to talk. This is like . . . like a foul ball after a full count. Things can go either way from here.*

"We think you remember things other people don't," KT said.

Evangeline laughed, a totally fake sound.

"Of course I remember things other people don't," Evangeline said. "Nobody could have my ac stats without an extraordinary memory."

She rolled her eyes at Max in a way that seemed to be trying to say, *You know what that's like, of course. Yeah, we're friends, you and me. Sorry your sister's such a loser.*

Don't you go trying to steal my teammate! KT wanted to snap at Evangeline. But she forced herself to take a deep breath and counter with a fake laugh of her own.

"I'm not talking about your memory for acs," KT said. "I mean, for real things. Real life. The real world. Don't you remember the real world?"

"You want to debate the meaning of reality?" Evangeline said. She flipped one of her stupid too-high pigtails over her shoulder. "I know what's real. And I know what *matters*. Can you make that same claim?"

"It doesn't matter what your hair looks like," KT said carefully. She looked at Evangeline's plaid jumper. "It doesn't matter what kind of clothes you want to wear. It doesn't matter if you're interested in things nobody else is interested in. I don't care about any of that."

"Well, thank you very much for giving me permission to be myself," Evangeline said mockingly. "Er—wait. Were you trying to get me to make fun of *you*? You're the different one. The things I like—mathletics, chemademics, poetry slam—those are the three top interests for middle-school-age kids *worldwide*. And I'm good at all of them. Makes me kind of . . . enviable, doesn't it?"

She knows, KT thought. *She knows everything.*

Angrily she kicked out her foot, snagging the wagon handle on the end of her shoe. She pulled it toward her, right into Evangeline's line of sight. KT didn't bother watching the other girl's face to see how she reacted. Instead KT reached down and cradled the bat and glove in her arms.

"KT!" Max exclaimed.

What's his problem? KT wondered. *Oh, does he really think I'd hit Evangeline with the bat?*

KT ignored him.

"You did this to us, didn't you?" KT asked, looking up at Evangeline, still behind the door. "To me. You shrank down everything that mattered to me in the whole world until it all fits in a little-kid wagon."

"It's not my fault if you're such a small person," Evangeline said, smirking.

"You know what I mean!" KT snarled. "You did this!"

"Evangeline! KT! Stop arguing!" Max surprised her by interrupting. "You two are the *same*. Evangeline, you really did write an anti-sports e-mail to the school administration in the real world, didn't you? And KT, you would have done the same thing if you were in Evangeline's shoes. The alt-world version of you *did*. My sister's acting like a total idiot, Evangeline, but if you really did manage to create this alternate reality yourself, both of us think you're a genius. Honest, we don't want to ruin anything for you. We both want you to be happy here—"

"But why do we have to be stuck here too?" KT interrupted, because Max was taking forever to get to the point.

Something shifted in Evangeline's expression, and for a second KT actually could see beyond the goofy hair and the oddball clothes and the weirdest-kid-in-school—maybe-even-in-*any*-school image.

Max is right, KT thought. *Evangeline and I really are alike. No matter what world either of us was in, no matter what anyone else thought of us, we'd still stay true to our real selves. But . . . we'd still want teammates. Both of us would.*

KT felt her own expression soften.

"Look," she said, and somehow all the anger had gone out of her now. She felt hope growing in its place. "I know what it felt like to be you, back in the real world. I've pretty much *been* you in this one. I'm really sorry if sports hurt you. I'm sorry if anything I ever did hurt you in any way. You do whatever you want to, for yourself. But can't you get Max and me back where we belong? Back to the real world?"

Evangeline stared out at KT and Max, the screen a mere shadow between them.

"You have a lot of confidence in me," she said slowly.

"Of course!" Max said, beaming. KT reached up and grabbed his arm, silencing him before he laid on any more exaggerated praise and delayed everything.

"Then you'll do it?" KT asked eagerly.

Evangeline kept gazing out the screen door. Strangely, it was KT she was peering at most intently.

"You aren't looking at the big picture," she said, shaking her head. She didn't exactly seem to be saying no. Her eyes kept boring into KT's. "Think about it. What makes you so sure you'd still be happy in the real world anyhow?"

Chapter twenty-one

KT was having memory problems again.

She woke in the dark in the middle of the night, her heart pounding frantically, prickles of dread running across her skin. She couldn't remember where she was.

Home, she told herself, looking toward the familiar glow of the clock on the nightstand, her softball glove beside it illuminated in the glow. *I'm home. I just had a bad dream.*

But she couldn't remember any dream. What was the last thing she could remember?

Standing on the porch at Evangeline's house, Evangeline saying, "What makes you so sure you'd still be happy in the real world anyhow?" And then . . . And then . . .

She found she could walk her memory forward from that moment. This wasn't like the last part of the Rysdale Invitational, which was completely absent from her mind. This was just hard to remember, because she'd felt so jolted.

Didn't Evangeline say after that, "Come back anytime,

Maxwell, if you want to work on math with me"? And then didn't she ease the door shut? And didn't I hear the pins falling into place in the door's lock, Evangeline locking out me and Max?

How could KT have heard that, when Evangeline's other words had taken over KT's brain?

What makes you so sure you'd still be happy in the real world anyhow?

What makes you so sure you'd still be happy in the real world anyhow?

What makes you so sure . . .

Max had looked back at KT, and through the din echoing in KT's head she'd heard him say, "What do you want to do now?"

And KT hadn't been able to say anything but "I need to go for a jog. I need to think."

She had gone running, but she hadn't let herself think. She'd been running away, trying not to think. She didn't want to wonder at Evangeline's words, didn't want to think about why going back to the real world might not make her happy after all. She'd run endlessly, wearing herself out. She'd gone to bed early.

And now she should just let herself sleep some more. It wasn't even morning yet. She shouldn't have to face anything until morning.

She closed her eyes to the darkness, and decided to forget about her tricky memory, forget about alt world, forget about Evangeline and her cryptic question. Instead KT pictured a beautiful spring day, the sun high overhead, a softball firm in her hand, a worthy batter facing her at home plate . . .

If you can see it, you can have it again, she told herself, revising her usual pre-game mantra only a little. *See it, have it. See it, have it . . .*

She fell asleep repeating those words to herself.

She woke up gasping. Gasping and gagging and sobbing . . . She rolled over and felt around on the nightstand for her softball glove, for comfort. She knocked over the alarm clock and a water bottle and her cell phone and iPod. She was clumsy because she wasn't picturing the nightstand right, the familiar arrangement of familiar objects. She was picturing some other nightstand, some other place.

She was picturing the nightstand from her bad dream. Or—was it still called a nightstand when it was a hospital's rolling table?

No! her mind screamed at her. *No! Don't think about that!*

But she couldn't stop herself. She remembered the bad dream now. She'd seen the same dream all over again, or she'd fallen back into it and lived through even more of it.

She'd been in a hospital bed, dim lights all around her except for the occasional pulsing glow of a monitor. Her parents were dark shapes beside her, and somehow she knew they were her real parents, the way they were supposed to be, not the horrible, crazy alt-world versions of them. They were talking in hushed tones, their voices mournful and low and only directed at each other, never KT. Did they think she was too sick or drugged to hear? Or was she too . . . damaged?

"If KT can't ever play softball again . . . ," Dad murmured sorrowfully.

And that was the moment when KT had gasped herself awake.

She scuttled across the bed like a frightened spider, drawing herself into the corner of the room, pressing her spine as hard as she could against the wall. She huddled there, arms wrapped around her legs, face buried against her knees. And still her thoughts rolled forward, completing her father's words.

If KT can't ever play softball again . . .

What if the rest of it was . . . *she wouldn't want anyone else to have it either?*

What if KT had conjured up this horrible world herself?

Chapter twenty-two

"No!" KT exploded.

The hall light outside her room came on; KT could see a dim glow under her door. There was a hushed rap of knuckles against her door.

"KT! Shh!" her mother's voice hissed at her. "I know you like to get up early, but you have to be quiet! Max has those tryouts today—he needs his sleep!"

Then KT heard Mom's footsteps recede, back toward her own bedroom.

Max! KT thought indignantly. *Of course it was all about Max! Did she even ask me what was wrong? Did she even stay for a second to make sure I was okay?*

The fury slammed through KT's body. But behind the anger was a wave of even more troubling questions.

What if things truly are bad now in the real world? What if . . .

No! KT wasn't going to let herself think like that. She

scrambled up, plucking her glove from the nightstand. She pulled a warm-up jacket and pants from the floor beside her bed, the motion sending the toppled alarm clock and iPod and cell phone tumbling across the rug. The alarm clock landed at a crazy angle, the numbers glowing upside down.

Did I break the clock? KT wondered. *Is that why it's showing two a.m. as zero-zero-backward-two?*

She remembered what her mother had said about getting up early—Mom wouldn't have said that if it was two a.m. KT's mind flipped the numbers around. Five. It was five in the morning.

That's when people get up who have a lot to do, KT thought. *But in this world I've got . . .*

She didn't let herself think the word "nothing." She was already moving, pulling on the pants and jacket, socks and shoes. Cradling her glove in her arms, she silently dashed out of her room, down the stairs, into the garage. She tugged the life-sized pitching mate and the basket of balls into the backyard. She positioned the pitching mate in the farthest corner of the yard. She stood there a moment too long, hugging the pitching mate.

No, no! she told herself. *Don't stop! Don't think! Don't . . .*

The word she was avoiding was "cry."

Focus! her brain screamed at her. *Practice! You've got to practice! Practice hard!*

She carried the basket of balls to the opposite corner of the yard and fired off the first throw, hard and quick. It landed perfectly in the netted center of the pitching mate.

Bull's-eye! She told herself. *Do it again! Throw fifty perfect pitches and then . . .*

Then what? What would she earn? What would she deserve?

Just focus on throwing the pitches.

Wasn't that what every coach she'd ever had would advise? Focus on the work before you started counting on the reward?

KT fired off ball after ball toward the pitching mate. She didn't have any way to measure it, but she told herself each throw had to be faster and faster and faster.

Fifty miles per hour, sixty, sixty-five . . . Could that last throw have maybe even been seventy miles per hour?

She made it to thirty perfect pitches, then had to start over because a ball went low and hit the rubberized base of the pitching mate before rolling off into the grass. She started her count back at the beginning.

One, two, three . . .

Perfect form, perfect arm, perfect throw. She was a *machine.*

Thirty-one, thirty-two, thirty-three . . .

At forty she paused to wipe sweat from her forehead with the back of her hand. Then she went back to throwing, as hard and fast and perfect as ever.

Forty-eight, forty-nine, fifty.

She hesitated. The sun was creeping over the horizon, bringing morning with it.

Fifty perfect throws was too easy, she told herself. *My goal should be one hundred.*

She went back to throwing and throwing and throwing.

Fifty-one, fifty-two, fifty-three . . . Sixty-eight, sixty-nine, seventy . . .

She was starting her eighty-ninth pitch when she heard a voice behind her.

"Stop! Please—just stop!"

Chapter Twenty-Three

KT's throw went wild, the ball missing the pitching mate by a good three feet. It sailed off into the shadows of the next yard.

KT whirled around to see who had ruined her perfect streak.

Max.

He stood at the edge of the patio, the toes of his bare feet dipping into the grass. Even in the dim light KT could see that he was wearing an old, stretched-out T-shirt that said MATH RULES! and shorts covered in large and small versions of the infinity symbol.

"Look what you made me do!" KT complained.

Max rubbed sleep out of his eyes.

"I know you think you're Superwoman," he said, his voice little-kid groggy. "But don't you ever worry that you might hurt yourself, doing all that?"

"No," KT said. "I never even get sore."

This was a lie, of course. Her legs ached from yesterday's excessive running; every time she moved her arm it throbbed, as if to complain about this morning's furious throwing.

KT remembered that yesterday morning she and Max had agreed to work together, to be teammates. She couldn't lie to him.

"At least," she corrected herself, "I never get so sore that I want to quit."

Max ambled forward and plopped down in the grass at KT's feet.

"Why is that, do you think?" he asked. "I mean, why are you so crazy, over-the-top obsessive about things, and I don't even care?"

KT sank down into the grass too.

"It'd be easier not to care," she said, trying to hold back the ache in her voice. "Nobody needs me to be like this, not in this world."

She had a brief flicker of wanting to tell Max about her dream, about her newest fears about the real world. But she couldn't have gotten the words out; she couldn't bear to think about any of that herself.

"Maybe, if you just got that crazy obsessive about math . . . ," Max began.

KT tried to consider this seriously. KT Sutton, mathletics star? Queen of the quotients, diva of the decimals . . .

She shook her head.

"It's not my thing," she said. "I could work at it forever and never be as good as Evangeline. Or—you."

She'd seen this in softball—girls who tried and tried and tried but lacked that easy muscle genius that came so naturally to KT and her club-team friends. Most of those less-talented girls got the message after a time or two of being cut in tryouts. They faded away, moved on to other activities, found some other skill to develop.

But that's not what should happen to me! KT thought fiercely. *I've got incredible softball talent! I should be allowed to use it! Not being able to—that's just not fair!*

It was like she was trying to argue with her father's words from her dream: *If KT can't ever play softball again . . .*

She couldn't think about that dream. She couldn't let herself hear those words again in her mind. Desperately, like a drowning swimmer flailing toward the only solid land in sight, she looked at Max.

Max is normal, she told herself. *Max is safe.*

But Max had such a stricken expression on his face. His jaw hung open. His eyes bugged out.

"You think I'm that good?" he asked. "Like, not just Mom and Dad bragging about me, building me up, the coach wanting me to play well, but—really good? *Evangeline* good?"

"Who got that last question in Friday's game, the one that really mattered?" KT asked. "You or Evangeline? Of course you're good! And"—she reached over and playfully punched his arm—"you know I wouldn't just say that to build you up. *I* wouldn't try to make you feel better about yourself!"

"Of course you wouldn't," Max said dazedly.

KT laughed. She was okay as long as she kept her gaze on Max's face. This was good, keeping her mind on Max's problems, not her own.

"But—," Max said hesitantly. "Shouldn't I actually *like* mathletics if I'm that good at it?"

"Maybe you would like it if you'd grown up playing it all along," KT said. "If you'd always thought math made you cool, not nerdy. But the way things were in the real world, well, I guess there your talent kind of got . . . overlooked."

Max picked up one of the softballs from the basket KT had been pitching from. He rolled it back and forth in his hand.

"Whose fault was that?" he asked. "Mom and Dad's? My teachers'? The school's?"

KT shrugged. Max was supposed to be her rescue, the only safe, normal person around. She couldn't have him acting all weird and troubled too.

"Calm down," she said, trying for her most soothing voice. "Why does any of that matter now? You're not in the real world anymore. You're here, where everybody knows about your talent. Everybody but you, I guess."

Max began tossing the ball from hand to hand.

"Everybody but me knows about my talent here; nobody but me knew in the real world," he said.

"What are you talking about?" KT said. Now she was confused. "I thought you said yesterday that you always just got in trouble in math class in the real world. Did you know you were good at it or not?"

Max made the ball fly faster and faster, traveling from hand to hand.

"I *should* have known," he said. "I kind of did, but I didn't want to. I ignored it. What did it matter, if the only thing Mom and Dad wanted me to be good at was sports? I wasn't paying attention to anything, really. A lot of times when I was playing video games I was just trying not to think about other things . . . hiding . . ." He snorted. "I was paying so little attention, you could have hit me in the head with a softball and I might not have even noticed!"

The ball rolled out of his hand and onto the grass.

Good old uncoordinated Max, KT thought, almost fondly. It was just so nice to have Max acting the way she expected him to.

But Max didn't sheepishly pick the ball back up and keep talking, the way she expected him to. He scrambled up and backed away from the ball, as if he was afraid of it.

"Is *that* what happened to send me here?" he asked. "At your softball game . . . could I have ignored everyone yelling 'heads up!' because a ball was coming into the stands? I could have . . . I did that all the time, because I figured Mom or Dad would stop the ball from hitting me if they had to. So I just kept playing my DS. . . ."

He had such a look of horror on his face. Horror—and the beginnings of understanding.

"But that day," he said. "That day, that game, that inning . . . Mom and Dad had gone out to stand at the railing because they were so excited, they wanted to get as close as possible. . . . I remember it all now! That *is* what happened! It must have made me black out when I got hit, and everything was different when I woke up. . . ."

"Max?" KT said, because he was scaring her. This was like watching some movie creature morphing into an entirely different life form. Max was still Max—same messy hair, same blobby face, same pudgy body, same math-themed T-shirt and shorts. But he was starting to stand up straighter now; he began looking down his nose at her instead of directly in the eye; his whole face had been taken over by . . . by . . .

Disgust.

"You woke me up with your stupid pitching, and you *know* I have mathletics club-team tryouts today!" he complained. It was heartbreaking how this could be so completely Max's voice, without sounding a thing like him. "If I make a single mistake today, it will be all your fault!"

He spun around and stomped away, each step as precise as a military maneuver.

"Wait!" KT yelled after him, her voice splintering. "You were telling me . . . What else do you remember from the real world?"

"This *is* the real world, you idiot!" Max snarled back at her without even breaking his stride. "Now be quiet and leave me alone!"

He reached the sliding glass door at the back of the house. He jerked it open, stepped inside, and yanked the door shut behind him.

He disappeared into the house.

KT, sitting alone in the grass, didn't move for a long time. She didn't let herself analyze what had just happened, what she'd just witnessed. But her brain put it together anyhow. This was the easiest thing she'd had to figure out since she'd opened her eyes Monday morning.

Max changed back, she thought numbly. *Real Max must have gotten zapped back to the real world somehow. That nasty kid at the end? That was the Max that really belongs here.*

But how could real Max have left without her?

Chapter Twenty-four

I still have Evangeline, KT finally thought, after a long while of searching desperately for something to buoy her up, something to hold on to. *Unless she's changed back now too.*

KT's mind darted away from that thought, trying to avoid it entirely.

If Evangeline's still on my team, I've got to let her know what happened, she told herself.

As far as KT knew, Evangeline was the only other person left in this crazy alternate world who might still remember the real world, her real self, and the real KT. But did that mean they were on the same team?

This wasn't like softball, where teams were clear-cut, color-coded. No matter who you played in softball, there were always only two sides: us and them.

This is more like . . . like one of those really big, really complicated tournaments, where you might root for or against teams in other brackets, because it affects who you'll play, how likely you are to win the championship, KT thought.

That didn't help. If she didn't know which team Evangeline was on, she sure didn't know what bracket she was in.

Knowing Evangeline, KT had a feeling she'd be in a category all her own.

Still, I've got to tell her about Max, KT thought. *It's what I'd want her to do for me.*

Besides, who else did KT have to confide in?

Stiffly, KT stood up and began gathering up softballs—the one Max had dropped, the one that had flown into the neighbors' yard, the pile trapped in the pitching mate's net. She was lugging the whole basketful back toward the garage when the sliding glass door by the patio slid open again.

"Make sure you pull that pitching-mate monstrosity back into the garage so it doesn't kill the grass," Mom called, poking her head out.

"I will," KT said dutifully, thinking, *Hate that alt-world Mom. Hate her!*

"We're about to leave to take Max to his club-team try-outs," Mom said. "It's at Brecksville South. We'll probably be there most of the day."

"Okay," KT said, thinking, *Alt-world Max was really exaggerating, saying I woke him up with my pitching. If they're leaving already, he would have had to get up early anyhow.*

Either that or KT had spent a lot of time sitting alone in the grass after he left her.

"This is only the biggest moment of Max's life, up to this point," Mom said. "It would be nice if you'd come in and wish him good luck. But I'm not going to make you if you can't do it sincerely."

What was KT supposed to say to that?

Mom hesitated for a moment, probably trying to make sure that KT got the full force of her glare. Then Mom started sliding the door shut.

"Wait!" KT cried, just before Mom had completely shut her out. "Do you know—is Evangeline Rangel going to be at the same tryouts?"

"Oh, so you *are* concerned about Max's competition?" Mom asked nastily. She kept the door open just a crack. "I guess that's something. . . . Yes, Evangeline will be there, but he won't have to worry about going up against her for the same spots. Because of the age cutoff, they're trying out for different teams."

"Okay. Thanks," KT said.

Mom narrowed her eyes at KT, but then just shut the door.

KT stayed in the backyard until she heard the garage door roll up and down and then the car engine hum off into the distance. She didn't think she could stand even looking at the new alt-world Max without wanting to punch him.

But . . . how he acted toward me . . . wasn't that pretty much how I usually acted toward him in the real world? some rebel part of her brain asked her.

She shoved that question over with all the others she was trying not to think about. Three years ago KT had had a coach who really liked making the girls run obstacle courses during practice, no matter how much they complained, "We're not football players. We're not soccer players. We don't usually have to dodge things during games. We just have to run fast. So *why* are you making us do this?"

As far as KT could remember, he never gave any better

answer than "because I said so." And then one of the girls had broken her ankle racing through rows of tires, and all the parents had complained, and that was the end of that.

KT had *hated* those obstacle courses. She believed running was for straight lines and precise angles: home to first to second to third to home. But now she felt like her brain had turned into that same kind of obstacle course, her mental censor constantly warning her: *No, wait—don't think about anything in this direction! You'll bump up against what Evangeline said yesterday, about how are you sure you'd still be happy in the real world anyhow . . . No! No! Not that direction either! You'll start thinking about last night's dream! . . . And whatever you do, don't start climbing any web of thoughts that goes from "Max ended up in alt world because he didn't notice something important" to "Was there something important that I failed to notice too? Or . . ." Stop! Come down from there! Think something else . . .*

Once again KT opted for action instead. She put the basket of balls and the pitching mate back into the garage. She took a shower, brushed her teeth, scarfed down a breakfast she could barely remember five minutes later. She called up directions to Brecksville South on her iPod: It was five miles away.

So that shower was a waste of time, she thought, lacing up her running shoes. *So what?*

She took off at a fast pace. The problem with running was that it was such a great accompaniment for thinking, and KT didn't want to think. She kept running faster and faster and faster, trying to outrun her own thoughts.

So when she arrived at Brecksville South, she was drenched

in sweat and panting hard. Tidy, prissy mathletes and their parents gave her startled glances as they streamed past her. A cluster of boys in starched oxford-cloth shirts and precisely ironed khakis waved their hands in front of their faces, as if trying to wave away the smell of her perspiration.

It's just good, honest sweat, KT thought, glaring back at them. *Get over yourselves.*

Still, she waited outside the school for a few minutes, trying to cool down before she went in to search for Evangeline. She fanned her soaked T-shirt back and forth; she smoothed back the sweaty tendrils of hair that had come loose from her ponytail; she pulled out and re-twisted her ponytail rubber band.

The constant stream of mathletes heading into the school slowed to a trickle and then stopped. From inside, KT heard a mechanized buzz, probably marking the start of a new tryout session.

No! KT thought. *Now I'll probably have to wait until Evangeline finishes this session. . . .*

She pushed her way through the front doors and came face to face with a trophy case that was even bigger than the one back at Brecksville North.

Chemademics champions three years in a row . . . Unbeaten in Geo-find four years in a row . . . The kids at this school must all be as scary-smart as Evangeline!

KT made herself look away. She followed the excited buzz of crowd noise down the hall toward a cafeteria. The room mostly contained parents conferring nervously over Styrofoam cups of coffee. But there were a few kids scattered here and there doing stress-relieving neck stretches or rattling off warm-up formulas. KT recognized the tension in the air, that combination of panic and fear and exhilaration and hope and dread that she'd always felt at softball tryouts. She felt herself getting keyed up just from the atmosphere.

"Are *you* here to try out?" a voice asked behind her.

KT turned around to see a pack of girls all wearing matching headbands, the wide swaths of fabric covered in numbers and mathematical symbols.

Really, you think that's cool? she thought. *Really?*

But there was such an air of menace in the way the three girls were standing, like they were warriors honor-bound to defend their turf from intruders like KT.

"N-no," KT found herself stammering. "I'm not trying out. I'm just here looking for a friend."

The girl at the front of the pack muttered something to the others—KT thought maybe it was "Someone like you would *never* find a friend here" or "Who'd want to be *your* friend?" or something like that. The other girls laughed.

"I hope you get cut in the first round," KT said. "I hope you flunk out of high school. I hope you're never academically eligible—I'm sorry, *athletically* eligible—to play your favorite ac in college."

She tossed her head, enjoying the thump of her sweaty ponytail against her back.

"How dare you—," the lead girl said, advancing toward KT.

"Is there a problem here?" a man asked, stepping between them.

"That girl threatened us!" the two sidekick girls complained in unison.

The man glanced at KT, then turned his back on her.

"Sabrina," he said. "Alexis. Katasha. Focus on the *math*. Don't get caught up in any tryout-day drama. Remember what happened the last time?"

KT walked away from all of them. She was surprised to find that her knees were shaking. She tried to flip around the whole scenario in her head.

If someone like Evangeline showed up at softball club-team tryouts in the real world, nobody would be mean to her, she thought. *Softball girls aren't nasty like that. Are we?*

It was yet another question she didn't want to think about.

KT walked toward a table with a huge sign taped to it proclaiming REGISTER HERE.

"Name?" the woman behind the table asked automatically without looking up.

"I'm not trying out," KT said. "I just want to know which room my, uh, friend is in so I can, uh, cheer her on. Can you look up Evangeline Rangel?"

Now the woman glanced at KT. She seemed to decide instantly that KT wasn't some whacked-out opponent of Evangeline's, like that one Olympic skater who'd arranged to have her top competitor's leg broken.

There are some definite advantages to looking like a straight-A student, KT thought.

"How nice that you support your friends in their acs!" the woman said in an overly sweet voice. She looked at a laptop screen. "Evangeline isn't in a tryout session right now, but she's already checked in, and she'll start in room 109 in twenty minutes. She's probably back there waiting. It's down that way, all right?"

She pointed, but the undertone in her voice seemed to be

saying, *I'm really not sure you're bright enough to follow that simple instruction. Not the way you look.*

"Thanks," KT said. She resisted the urge to tell this woman, *I hope your kid washes out at these tryouts. I hope your kid flunks out of high school. I hope your kid never gets to play acs in college.* KT already had enough problems as it was.

She headed down the hallway. It probably wouldn't be a good idea to run into Mom or Dad or Max, so she ducked her head down and turned her face to the side every time she passed a classroom. Still, she could hear the voices spilling out of each room, confident or trembling, filled with fear or hope: "4x over 3 . . ." "Cosine—er, no, I mean tangent . . ." "The area of that rhombus would be . . ."

Not my scene, KT thought, with a little pang in her heart. *Not my people. Not my tribe.*

Such a loud burst of applause came from one room as she passed that KT couldn't resist peeking in. She almost fell over in surprise at the sight of the kids lined up in the front of the room. KT stood there gaping for a moment, then tugged on the sleeve of an official-looking man standing with a clipboard by the door.

"That . . . that girl with 'sixty-four' pinned to her shirt . . . is that girl named Chelisha?" she asked.

The man laughed.

"Oh, yeah," he said. "You've heard of her, have you? She's the most amazing mathlete I've ever seen. But don't worry—nobody here's actually competing with her today. They just brought her in to let everyone see what the kids from this region might eventually be up against, if anyone gets that far. The play in this room is strictly for exhibition purposes."

This Chelisha was wearing horn-rimmed glasses and the same kind of "Nerds 'R' Us" combination of plaid and argyle as the other mathletes around her. But KT knew it had to be the same amazing batter she'd faced across home plate at the Rysdale Invitational back in the real world. As KT watched, Chelisha bowed her head slightly, accepting the applause. Obviously it was all for her.

"She . . . she . . . ," KT stammered.

"Hey, don't let it get to you," the man with the clipboard. "Personally, I think it was a mistake bringing her in today—nerves are already running high enough—but, really, she's in a class by herself, so you can't take it personally." He glanced again at KT. "I hear she's a really good student, too, so her college scholarship is guaranteed!"

KT backed away from the man, out of Chelisha's room. Her head spun. It felt like worlds were colliding.

It's not fair for Chelisha to be great at math and *softball,* KT thought. *It means she can be happy in both worlds. And if Evangeline is right, I can't be happy in either.*

KT didn't want to think about that. She stumbled to the left, as if physically trying to dodge the thought. But this just made her slam into the hallway wall. She was so dizzy. She let herself slide down the wall into a crouch.

"Not fair," she murmured. "Not fair for her to have so many talents! Not when I only have one!"

"How can you be so sure?" a voice said above her, echoing oddly in KT's ringing ears. "When have you ever given anything but softball a chance?"

Softball! KT thought. *Somebody here in this crazy, sports-forsaken alt world actually said the word 'softball'!*

She looked up eagerly, sending herself into another spiral of dizziness. It took a long moment for the face looking down on her to swing into focus. And when it did, disappointment slammed through KT.

It was only Evangeline.

Behind Evangeline, other people were starting to crowd in, asking, "Did she faint?" "Do we need to call an ambulance?" "Have you sent someone for orange juice? If her blood sugar's low, orange juice will help" and "Can't she handle the pressure?"

Evangeline waved them all away.

"She's fine! Just give her some air—and some privacy! What are you, a bunch of vultures?"

She spoke so authoritatively that in seconds the crowd melted away, and KT and Evangeline were left alone in the hall.

KT blinked up at the other girl.

"You are . . . on my team," KT said. "We're on the same side."

"Well, duh," Evangeline said, shaking her twin pigtails back away from her face. "Couldn't you tell that yesterday?"

Chapter Twenty-five

KT sat up a little straighter, outrage winning out over the dizziness.

"No, Evangeline, I couldn't tell that yesterday," she said. "All you did yesterday was make bizarro comments and tell me I couldn't be happy. And then you shut the door in my face."

"I didn't tell you you couldn't be happy," Evangeline said, sitting down beside her. "I said—"

"I know what you said!" KT exclaimed. She didn't want to hear it again. "I was—what's it called?—paraphrasing."

"Well, you really should paraphrase accurately," Evangeline said prissily. "Sloppy thinking can lead to all sorts of disasters and tragedies."

"Like me getting sent here?" KT asked.

Evangeline fixed her with a steady look.

"When you step back and look at the big picture," she said slowly, "you may have a totally different view of your own particular tragedy."

My own tragedy? KT wanted to say. *Are you saying that there's more to it than this?*

But she couldn't ask that, because what if Evangeline answered?

"It's really hard to follow what you're saying," KT complained instead.

"I get that a lot," Evangeline admitted. "Even in this world." She bit her lip. "I really would have thought it'd be different here."

Is Evangeline admitting that she did create this world? KT wondered. *And that she made mistakes? Is it her fault that I'm here? Am I feeling guilty for nothing?*

Somehow KT couldn't bring herself to ask any of these questions either.

She swiped her hand across her forehead, wiping away clamminess this time, not sweat.

"There's a girl in there," she began, pointing toward the room she'd just left. "Chelisha. In the real world she's an awesome batter, and she was the last batter I faced before blacking out and waking up in this wacko world. Should I go say something to her? Ask her to send me back? Is she the key to me getting home?"

Evangeline frowned and shook her head.

"You don't listen very well, do you?" she asked. "Are you even paying attention? This isn't about Chelisha."

Paying attention, KT thought. *Max talked about paying attention. . . .*

She remembered that she'd originally come here to tell Evangeline about Max.

"Max found his way home," she said. "Back to the real

world. At least—I'm pretty sure that's what happened. He's all right, don't you think?"

She hadn't realized she was going to ask that.

"I think Max had the best chance of any of us for getting back safely," Evangeline said. "I think he had the least to overcome."

This wasn't what KT would have expected Evangeline to say.

"Well, if you want to follow after him, I saw him make the change, and I think I know what happened," KT said. "He figured out how he got here in the first place, and, boom! Just like that he switched back."

"ENNH," Evangeline said, making a sound like a buzzer in mathletics. "Your hypothesis is incorrect."

"It's not a hypothesis!" KT insisted. "It's fact! It's observation! It's . . ." She sighed. "Why do you think I'm wrong?"

"Think, KT," Evangeline said.

That was the last thing KT wanted to do.

Now it was Evangeline's turn to sigh. She leaned back against the wall.

"I know you're wrong," she began, "because I also figured out how I got here in the first place. But did *I* change back? No. Two test subjects, same variable, different results—ergo—"

"Don't turn this into a science problem!" KT complained. "This is real life I'm talking about!"

"Hmm. That may not be the first 'given' you want to start with," Evangeline said. "In science you need to test every assumption—"

"Stop it! Speak English!" KT commanded. "If I'm so wrong, how do *you* think Max got out of here?"

"Okay, okay!" Evangeline said, waving her hands defensively in front of her. "Here's what I think: It's not enough to *remember* what got you here. You must also *accept* what got you here."

KT opened her mouth to argue. Then she shut it. She remembered the expression on Max's face that morning when he'd cried out, *I remember it all now! That* is *what happened!*

"He got hit in the head with a softball at one of my games," KT said.

"See? Not such a terrible thing to have to accept," Evangeline said gently. "As long as the ball wasn't moving too fast."

KT squirmed uncomfortably, suddenly aware of how hard the floor was beneath her.

What if . . .

She didn't let herself finish the thought.

"I think mostly Max just felt stupid that he let the ball hit him," KT said, filling in the silence. "Because he was zoning out, playing some idiotic handheld game . . ."

"I see," Evangeline said. "Stupid, yeah, but hopefully not tragic."

KT didn't like that word echoing between them: *tragic, tragic . . .*

"So if you know so much, what'd you do to get here?" KT asked. "Let me guess, what's tragic for someone like you? Oh, I know—did you get a ninety-nine instead of one hundred on some test? Or, wait, coming here must have been a reward for you, a prize, so—"

"No," Evangeline said, her voice slashing across KT's rush of words. "This is pretty much torture for me. Because I know it isn't real. Because it reminds me again and again what I'll probably never have, because of what I did."

"Which was?" KT asked.

Evangeline looked down. After a moment she let out a soft sigh.

"I did write an e-mail to the principal and the athletic director and all the teachers and coaches," she began slowly. "And after that, it wasn't just kids who acted mean to me. It was, like, some of the adults turned on me, too, you know?"

"I know," KT said grimly. "The same thing happened to me in this world."

Evangeline dipped her head farther down and then back up, accepting this.

"I was desperate," Evangeline said. "I started using faulty logic. I thought, if my problem is that I'm too smart for everyone, I just . . . won't be that smart. So I flunked this big math test on purpose, something that's going to go on my high school record—"

"Because you're taking classes years ahead of everyone else," KT said. "Right?"

Evangeline nodded again. Her shoulders slumped, as if bowed by shame.

"As soon as I walked out of that test, I knew I'd made a big mistake. The kind of colleges I'd want to go to—MIT, Caltech, Harvard, places like that—it's not enough to be a genius. You have to be a genius *and* perfect!" Evangeline said.

"Couldn't you have just talked to the teacher? Retaken the test?" KT asked.

"Not in that class," Evangeline muttered.

KT guessed the standards for grades in high school must be higher than in middle school.

"Then couldn't you just retake the class and replace the

grade?" KT asked. "Maybe you'd be a little bored, and you'd just be two years ahead instead of three, but—good grief! You're only in seventh grade! How could a college expect you to already be perfect by seventh grade?"

"Where were you when I needed all this good advice?" Evangeline asked, and it only halfway seemed as though she was joking.

"Probably out on some softball field," KT muttered. "But hey, I've got your back now! There—problem solved!"

Evangeline shook her head.

"That's not the end of it," she said grimly. "That afternoon I went home, and I was so upset I started a chemistry experiment in the garage to cheer myself up."

KT decided not to point out that this was hardly the typical seventh-grader pick-me-up. She looked around.

"So you created this whole alternate world as a science experiment in your garage to cheer yourself up?" she asked.

"No, no—*listen*," Evangeline said. But it was a moment before she went on. And when she did, her voice was different, as if every word she spoke threatened to choke her. "I don't know, I guess I was too angry to measure everything carefully. I wasn't thinking clearly. I was in no condition to work with dangerous chemicals. Because what happened after that was . . . I kind of . . . I blew up the whole garage."

KT gasped.

"Were you okay?" she asked.

Evangeline flashed her a disgusted look.

"The garage roof fell on me," she said. "How could I possibly have been okay? Would I have ended up here if everything was okay?"

Evangeline didn't create this world, KT thought. *At least— not on purpose. Not any more than I did.*

"So you know all this about how you got here, and, and . . . you're fighting with everything you've got *not* to go back home, aren't you?" KT asked.

"Exactly," Evangeline said. "What if it turns out that I injured my brain somehow? All I ever was, was smart. What if it turns out that I'm not even smart anymore, back in the real world?"

And, KT thought, *what if it turns out that I . . .*

KT shut down this line of reasoning instantly.

"So you can just live the rest of your life in this alternate world," KT offered Evangeline. "You're happy here. It's designed just for you! You're the star!"

"KT," Evangeline said gently, "this isn't a real place. I'm not sure how much longer it can last. For either of us."

KT didn't have anything to say to that.

A man with a clipboard walked down the hallway.

"Three-minute warning!" he called out. "Three minutes until the next tryout session starts!"

Evangeline darted forward, surprising KT by drawing her into a hug. Then she let go.

"You know, I was kind of jealous of you, back in the real world," Evangeline admitted. "Sometimes I watched you and your friends in the school cafeteria . . ."

"What? Why?" KT asked, stunned all over again. "I wasn't that popular. I wasn't like the cheerleaders and the football players or, I don't know, the student-body president. I wasn't even that smart!"

"Oh, the cheerleaders and the football players and the

student-body president were miserable—why would I be jealous of them?" Evangeline said. "I watched them, too, and you could tell. They were always worried about what other people thought of them. They were always trying to be somebody they weren't—skinnier or prettier or funnier. . . . You didn't care what anybody thought. You were just happy being yourself."

"I was always trying to be a better softball player," KT corrected her. "I wasn't happy unless I won."

Evangeline laughed.

"Well, you almost always won, didn't you? That's all I saw," she said. She stood up. "Come talk to me after tryouts. I mean, if you're still here."

KT felt dizzier than ever.

If you're still here, if you're still here, if you're still here . . .

Where else could she possibly go?

Chapter Twenty-six

Evangeline turned away and started walking toward room 109. Kids and parents began pouring out of the other classrooms, switching between tryout sessions.

Can't stay in this hallway, KT thought dazedly. *Might run into Mom or Dad or that awful version of Max.*

She couldn't face any of them right now.

She sprinted into a side hallway that didn't seem to be in use. She dashed all the way down to the end and pushed out the door. She was behind the school now.

KT had been to Brecksville South before for softball games, and it was almost as big of a jolt here as at her own school to see a blank, open lawn where the sports fields were supposed to be. KT took off running: running away from the missing softball diamond and the missing soccer fields and the missing football stadium and track; running away from everything Evangeline had told her; running away from everything she didn't want to figure out on her own.

Somehow it had gotten colder since KT had last been out-side—evidently it was going to be one of those days where the temperature dropped all day long. Stepping in and out of shadows, KT could feel the pale, weak sunshine trying to warm things up, and completely failing.

Oh, well, it's not even spring yet, KT thought. *But we're almost there. And spring's always the best time to play softball . . .*

Except, maybe not this year. If what Evangeline said was true—if what KT herself was trying not to think was true—then KT might not even get to play softball this spring. Not at all. Not even if she found her way back to the real world.

No! KT thought, almost doubling over in pain. *No!*

She straightened up, put on a burst of speed.

That thought had sneaked up on her. She wasn't going to let that happen again.

I'll . . . I'll try again to come up with a way to play softball here in this world, KT thought. *I won't use Facebook this time where I ruined things by sounding creepy. I'll go old-school— I'll put signs up all over town. I'll send letters to all the middle schools in the area. Maybe to the high schools too. That'll work!*

But she could hear Evangeline's voice echoing in her head, saying: *This isn't a real place. I'm not sure how much longer it can last. For either of us.* No matter how hard KT tried, it was possible that she wouldn't get a chance to play softball here. She might run out of time.

But this world feels real! KT told herself. *I have on real running shoes! My feet are pounding real pavement!*

And yet as soon as she thought that, everything around her started seeming less real. In reality you didn't have to keep reminding yourself what was real. More and more, her easy strides felt like running in a dream. The scenery flowing past her—houses, trees, grass, street, cars—seemed blurry and indistinct.

And . . . slightly unreal.

KT's pace flagged. In her mind she let herself inch toward one of the forbidden obstacles, one of the thoughts she'd been trying not to think.

How bad could things actually be in the real world? she thought. She let herself remember the flash she'd gotten again and again, the sense that she'd been hurt somehow, was maybe even in the hospital. *Even if it's a broken bone— bones heal. Athletes get injured all the time. And sure, they might have to miss some practices and games—or even a whole season—and that's awful, but they go through rehab and physical therapy and then they're back, good as new.*

Even if it was something truly horrible—even if KT had been in some sort of accident where she'd lost a limb, an arm or a leg—well, even that wouldn't stop her from playing softball. She'd just become a standout wheelchair athlete, or she'd be like that baseball pitcher who lost his right arm to cancer and started pitching left-handed instead.

How could I have lost an arm or a leg? KT wondered. *The last thing I remember in the real world, all I was doing was throwing a ball.*

Her mind skittered away from that thought, and she started running faster again, so fast she didn't have room in her mind for anything but *Stride forward. Pump your arms. Run! Run! Run!*

An unwanted thought crept in anyway.

What if I wasn't the one who got terribly hurt?

Would a girl get banned from the game if she'd thrown a soft-ball that maimed or even killed her little brother? If that happened, even if she was allowed, would she ever want to play again?

KT tripped on a crack in the sidewalk and plunged forward. She was going too fast to catch herself, but she fell crooked and started sliding. The rough cement underneath her scraped all along her right arm and leg.

"Blood," KT whispered, looking down at her arm. "Real blood."

She wanted to think about that, wanted to concentrate on pressing her T-shirt against the wounds, holding her arm up until the bleeding stopped. But a whole scenario had unfolded in her mind right before she tripped, and KT found that she couldn't push it out again.

Max was certain that he'd been hit in the head with a softball at the Rysdale Invitational championship game. He knew that that was what sent him into this alternate world. And I know that, right before I blacked out, I threw a ball. It was supposed to go to first base, but it was a wild throw. What if my throw went into the stands? What if it hit Max?

KT remembered what Evangeline had said about Max getting hit: *Not such a terrible thing to have to accept. As long as the ball wasn't moving too fast.*

KT threw *hard*.

Evangeline didn't act like Max had really been in any great danger, KT reminded herself, trying to calm herself down. *She said Max had the least to overcome of any of us.*

But Evangeline didn't know much about softball. She was probably fooled by the name: Softballs weren't actually all that soft. There had been cases of people hit by softballs getting seriously injured or even killed.

Mostly pitchers, KT told herself, even as her heart beat faster. *Pitchers standing at close range, right in front of a ball flying out from a bat after a really hard hit . . .*

A batted ball could go so much faster than one thrown accidentally into the stands.

It'd be such a freaky accident, to have Max get seriously hurt from my throw, KT told herself.

But freaky things happened. Hadn't this last week proved that to KT?

This past week wasn't real, she told herself, and it was strange how that had become a comforting thought.

Wasn't it freaky to begin with that KT had been so incredibly good at softball? Didn't that prove that really unlikely things could happen?

Even though she was still bleeding, KT scrambled up and started running again. But she couldn't seem to get up enough speed to outrun anything anymore.

In that dream I had—Dad wasn't saying anything about Max being hurt, KT told herself. *He was saying, "If KT can't play softball ever again . . ."*

What if Dad hadn't been talking about a physical problem? What if he meant, psychologically, that she'd never be able to play again?

It's just a game, KT told herself. *I'd give it up in a heartbeat if it meant nothing bad really happened to Max.*

KT was surprised to find that thought in her brain—it was something else that had just crept up on her.

But it's true, isn't it? she thought in wonderment. *Wouldn't I give up softball if I had to, to save Max's life?*

KT wouldn't have even thought to ponder such a dilemma

before. Softball had always just automatically mattered more than anything else.

Oh, please. Don't let that be the choice, KT thought.

She realized she was trying to bargain with God, or whoever was in control of the real world—or both worlds. But what good was that? Even if she'd played some role in conjuring up this alternate universe, she couldn't control it. And, she knew now, neither could Evangeline.

KT tried to run faster, but everything around her had taken on the slow-motion quality of a dream. And, just like in dreams, the people around her weren't acting normal. Here she was, racing down the sidewalk, dripping blood—maybe even gasping and screaming a little too—and not a single person tried to stop or help her: not dog walkers, not moms pushing strollers, not dads carrying bags of groceries, not teenagers holding up signs about car-wash fund-raisers . . . Everyone just stepped aside, letting her pass. It was like they all knew she was already headed wherever she needed to go.

KT didn't have the slightest idea where she was going. She didn't know this street; she was just running blindly. She glanced around as she turned a corner, entering a section of the city that wasn't set up well for a solitary runner. The buildings were too big; the streets were too wide; the traffic moved too fast. And some of the vehicles that zoomed past were topped with red lights that flashed distractingly . . .

Ambulances, KT thought.

She was running toward the hospital.

The Brecksville Memorial Hospital complex sprawled at the top of a hill, looking urgent and scary and more real than anything else around her.

KT stopped, staring up at the glowing EMERGENCY sign. Blurry shapes moved around her—hospital workers arriving for a shift change, maybe? Because she didn't want to look at the hospital, she tried to look at these people instead, but they were ghostly, wavering, barely there.

Of course, KT thought. *More proof that this world isn't real. How could the hospital function if 99.9 percent of grown-ups in this world work at nothing but exercise? How could any business work? How could people have food and clothes and houses?*

She realized that very little about this alternate world made sense past the middle-school scene. The e-mail that she—and/or Evangeline—had written was right: School really was supposed to get kids ready to be adults, with adult jobs. What kids learned in school needed to be more important than the games they played outside of it.

As soon as she thought that, the blurry shapes around her fell away. Everything started falling away except the hospital in front of her.

KT began running toward it.

Evangeline knew what she was talking about, she thought. She felt a pang, because she wasn't going to be able to go back and talk to Evangeline about this. Or maybe that was just her heart and lungs threatening to burst, because she was trying so hard to run fast enough to escape the wreckage caving in on her. *This world was never anything but temporary. Just a place to hide while we avoided facing the real world.*

The sliding glass doors of the hospital lobby slid open before KT.

Almost there, almost there . . .

At the last minute, right at the edge of the threshold, KT dug her heels in, leaned back, drew herself to an abrupt stop.

Immediately everything stopped falling around her. Everything stopped, period.

KT stood there panting.

"So I still have some control?" she whispered. "I still have some choice in the matter?"

She stood on a single concrete square of sidewalk—the only square that hadn't fallen away into nothingness. In fact it was the only thing outside of the hospital that was still intact.

I don't have to go into that hospital, KT thought defiantly. *I could just stay here.*

She glanced back at the collapsed world behind her. The blur of broken scenery seemed to be making a feeble attempt to reassemble—if she squinted hard enough, she could almost make herself see the street, the cars, the trees, the grass. She might be able to bring the whole fake world back. She might be able to make herself believe in it.

But what good would that do? she asked herself. *What good is any of it, if it's all just a lie? And—how could I go on like this, never knowing the truth? Never knowing how everything turned out in the real world for Max? Or . . . me?*

She turned her back on the fake world. She stared down at the metal strip at the base of the hospital doorway. The glass doors still hung open, waiting.

"I don't know how much control I'll have over anything else," she said aloud. "But I get to decide about this. And this is my choice: I want to know."

She squared her shoulders and stepped across the threshold. The hospital doors slid shut behind her.

Chapter twenty-seven

Darkness engulfed her.

At first KT thought all her senses had given out on her, overwhelmed by the strain of running toward the hospital, of making her decision. But dimly, distantly, she could actually hear a steady noise.

Beep . . . beep . . . beep . . .

She struggled to open her eyes.

Eyelids . . . so heavy, she thought, barely managing an eyelash flutter.

"She's coming to!" someone cried. "She's waking up!"

Dad's voice, KT thought. *Dad.*

With what seemed like superhuman effort, KT lifted her eyelids just enough that Dad's face swam into focus.

Real Dad, KT thought, just from the one brief glimpse she got before her eyes slid shut again. There was something in his face—pride? Wonder?—that had been mostly absent every time he'd looked at her in the other world. But it was mixed with worry and exhaustion and something she'd seen on his face a lot in alt world.

Is it . . . pity? KT thought. *For me? Not because I'm a misfit in an ac-obsessed world but because . . . because of what happened at the Rysdale Invitational?*

"KT, honey, take it easy," Mom's voice came from nearby. She must be sitting right beside Dad. "Don't push yourself too hard. You can wake up slowly."

KT shook her head, feeling some sort of rough pillowcase against her cheeks, her hair flailing against her left shoulder.

"Have to know . . . Max . . . Is Max okay?" she murmured.

"See, I told you she didn't hear what we tried to tell her." Mom's voice sounded muffled. Evidently she'd turned her head to talk to Dad.

"Max . . . hurt," KT whispered. "My fault . . . I hurt him . . ."

"Oh, bless her heart, the first thing she's worried about is Max," Mom said.

"But is he—," KT began.

"Max is fine, honey," Dad said in a booming voice, as if he knew he had to talk loudly to get through to KT. She felt like her ears and her brain had been stuffed with cotton. "They were afraid he might have a mild concussion, and they kept him in the hospital for observation overnight, but it was just a precaution. He doesn't even have a headache anymore."

"I . . . hit him," KT whispered. "My throw . . ."

"Nobody blames you for that, KT, not even Max," Mom said. "It was such a fluke, the way that ball bounced off the railing . . . Believe me, you don't have to worry about Max. "

"Oh. Okay," KT said, relaxing back into the darkness, back into the scratchy sheets and pillow beneath her.

Relief flowed through her.

I got all upset for nothing, she thought, snuggling deeper into the blankets and sheets. *Everything's fine. Isn't that what Mom and Dad just said?*

She could still hear the steady beeping, like some sort of monitor measuring somebody's heartbeat. Why would the hospital still have a monitor running if Max didn't even have a headache?

Mom and Dad didn't say that everything was fine, KT realized. *They said that* Max *was fine.*

KT went back to struggling to open her eyes. She was still trying to make sense of how she'd gotten from stepping into the hospital lobby in the alternate world to here, wherever here was.

I must have been zapped back to wherever I'm supposed to be in the real world right now, she thought. *Wherever I ended up after blacking out at the Rysdale Invitational . . .*

The electronic beeping seemed to get louder, more urgent: *Beep . . . beep . . . beep . . .*

"KT, honey, don't get agitated," Mom said. "You need to stay calm."

Why? KT wondered.

She managed a blink, and got another quick glimpse of Dad—and Mom—hovering over her. Beyond them she could see a fluorescent panel of light, the top of an IV pole, and a remote control with a call light labeled NURSE.

Hospital room, KT thought. *And—am I the one lying in the hospital bed?*

She tried to push her way up—maybe her eyelids would work better if she was in an upright position. But her right arm seemed to be immobilized. And trying to move it sent out little shivers of almost pain. It was like her arm wanted to scream out, DON'T DO THAT! IT'LL REALLY HURT! but there was some blessed numbness blocking the sensation.

"KT, honey, just lie still," Mom begged. She pushed down on KT's left shoulder, holding her in place.

KT got her eyes completely open. She looked down at her right arm, her pitching arm. It was encased in an unwieldy brace. Someone had evidently decided that it had to be kept absolutely still.

KT squinted at the brace, completely baffled.

"What? Why—?" she began.

"Oh, Bill, she doesn't remember that, either," Mom moaned.

"You tore your rotator cuff," Dad said, still with the same overly loud, overly careful voice he'd used before. "The muscles and tendons in your shoulder. The doctors said you must have had some serious overuse problems before the Rysdale championship game, and then—"

"Torn rotator cuff? Is that all?" KT interrupted. It wasn't just relief that flowed through her this time—it was practically glee. This was bad, and a week ago she would have considered it the greatest tragedy of her life. But it was nothing like the unbearable possibilities that she'd been imagining; it was nothing like being stuck in a world without softball. Rotator-cuff injuries weren't all that uncommon for pitchers. She could handle this. She could even be noble about it.

"How long will it take to heal?" she asked, trying to sound patient. "How many games will I have to sit out?"

Mom and Dad exchanged glances.

"Well . . . ," Dad said.

"KT, honey, wouldn't you rather rest some more before we talk about all of this?" Mom said in a choked voice. "You've already been through a lot."

KT looked back and forth between her parents. Her mother had tears in her eyes.

If I close my eyes, could I go back to the other world? KT wondered. *Is it too late to change my mind?*

She thought it probably was.

"There's something else, isn't there?" KT asked quietly. "Something you're not telling me."

Dad clutched KT's left hand.

"Oh, KT," he said, his voice breaking.

"You have to tell me," KT said. "Was it the rotator-cuff surgery—have I had surgery yet? Did something go wrong?"

Dad pressed KT's left hand against his cheek.

"Not wrong, but . . . ," he began.

"There was a complication," Mom said. "The way you passed out during the game . . . They wanted to check you out a little more thoroughly."

"Did I hit *my* head?" KT asked. She almost giggled, because there would have been a certain justice to that, her getting a concussion at the same time that she gave Max one. "You told them I need my shoulder back in shape as soon as possible, didn't you? They know I'm a pitcher, right?"

Another look passed between Mom and Dad, which KT could read only as *This is bad. This is really bad.*

"Right?" KT said, panic started to edge into her voice. "They know?"

KT wouldn't have thought it was possible, but Mom and Dad's faces hardened even further into grimness.

"We really don't have to talk about this right now," Mom said, making an attempt at briskness. Her voice broke. "Just—"

"Tell me!" KT commanded. "Tell me, or I will get agitated, I won't rest, I'll make my shoulder even worse . . ."

She started to squirm out of bed—not because she wanted to hurt her shoulder, but because she wanted to show them what she was still capable of. Even with her arm in a brace, she was still KT Sutton, pitcher. She could still control the game.

Couldn't she?

Mom and Dad both grabbed her left arm, pulling her back into place.

"We *have* to tell her," Dad said. "We have to, or else she'll be out trying to run laps around the hospital corridors at night."

Why did he sound so sad about that? This was the real world again, wasn't it? This was Real Dad, who was supposed to be bursting with pride over his athletic daughter.

What was wrong with him?

Dad began staring fixedly down at his own hands, holding KT down.

"They did some tests," he began. "They found some . . . problems with your heart . . . problems we'd never known about. Problems you must have had all your life, but . . ."

"Sometimes they get worse in adolescence," Mom whispered.

"Oh, but who cares, if it never bothered me?" KT said, doing her best to shrug in spite of the brace on her right shoulder. Whatever numbing agent she had working on her shoulder seemed to be working on her mind, too. She felt perfectly calm.

"I wasn't going to tell you this, but it *really* hurt when I was throwing that ball at the Rysdale Championship. I'm sure it was just the pain that made me pass out. Who won, anyway?"

"KT, they stopped the game because everyone was so worried about you," Dad said. "You and Max, both . . ."

"People have died because of the heart problems you have," Mom said. "*You* could have died!"

"But I didn't," KT said, still fighting to sound calm. She felt a chill swimming out from her heart, but she did her best to ignore it. "Now that they know about this heart thing, they'll take care of it, and I'll be fine, right?"

"Right," Mom said. "It absolutely can be controlled with medication and monitoring and . . . lifestyle changes."

She sounded like a medical manual.

"So, see," KT said, "I can so run laps—"

"No!" Mom and Dad exclaimed together.

There was such panic in their voices. Panic and fear and sorrow and regret . . . It was like someone had died, like they'd lost their home, like everything they'd always believed in and counted on and hoped for had turned into dust.

KT thought she could feel her heart beating in the silence that fell over the room just then.

"Why not?" she whispered.

"It's not safe for you to do any . . . extreme exercise," Dad said, and his voice sounded like it was him falling apart, him fighting against devastating pain. "Anything much more than a brisk walk . . . it's too dangerous."

"How long will that last?" KT asked. She was trying so, so hard to keep from wailing. "How long until I can get back to softball?"

Neither of her parents answered her. Neither of them would look her in the eye. Tears streamed down both of their faces.

KT had never seen her father cry before.

"Will I ever get to play softball again?" KT whimpered.

"You—," Dad began.

"They can't guarantee—," Mom began.

And then, almost as if they were mirror images of the same person, Mom and Dad bounded up and fled the room. KT could hear her mother's racking sobs echoing down the hall.

They can't take it, KT thought. *They can't bear to say the words. They ran away instead of telling me.*

And KT couldn't even get up and run after them. She couldn't run away from anything anymore. She lay completely still, as if her heart would stop if she so much as moved. She'd been wrong: There was no painkiller working on her brain. Or if there was, it was worthless, the equivalent of a baby aspirin trying to fight a massive tumor.

This is what I was trying to hide from in the alternate world, KT thought. *This is what sent me there.*

Mom and Dad had probably tried to tell her before. Tried and failed. She had no idea how much time had passed in the real world since the Rysdale Invitational championship. She felt like things were once again falling apart, but it was everything ahead of her that was collapsing now, not just scenery she'd already passed.

There'd be no Brecksville North eighth-grade season of perfect shutout games. No KT Sutton commemorative jersey in the school trophy case. No eighth-grade season at all. Not for KT.

There'd be no glorious high-school triumphs on some amazing club team including the best softball players from a four- or five-hour radius.

There'd be no national championship games, no college recruiters offering scholarships. No University of Arizona. No Olympics, no World Cup, no gold medals. No medals at all.

No softball at all.

No running.

Nothing.

KT had nothing left anymore.

Will I even live? KT wondered. *Could I drop dead just from the strain of lying here trying to breathe?*

How could Mom and Dad have left her to deal with all of this alone?

She heard a sniffle across the room. She whipped her head to the right: It was Max. He was sitting in one of the hospital chairs, his head bowed—the same posture he always had, hunched over some video game.

I came back for you! KT wanted to yell at him. *I came back because I wanted to make sure you were okay, and I just got the worst news of my life—and you're just sitting there playing a video game?*

Then KT realized he wasn't actually playing a video game. His hands were empty. It was more like he had his head bowed to give her privacy, to give her space. Maybe he was even praying for her.

While KT was staring at Max, he suddenly raised his head. Their eyes met, and it was incredibly weird. She wasn't used to looking into her brother's eyes. She couldn't remember the last time she'd done it—not for real, not outside the alternate world.

"At least . . . ," Max began faintly. "At least you still have your team."

"Oh, yeah, I'm sure all the girls will rally around me," KT said. But there was already a bitter edge to her voice.

It won't last long, she thought. She could picture her friends—Vanessa and Bree, Molly and Lex—all visiting the hospital, making strained chitchat, then running out with the cruel excuse, "Sorry! Gotta go! Big game today!"

How many times would they even bother coming?

"Not that team," Max said, wrinkling his nose. "I mean . . . you and me. And . . . Evangeline?"

KT gaped at him. She blinked hard.

"You remember?" she whispered.

Chapter Twenty-eight

"There was another world," Max said cautiously.

"You were some great mathlete and I couldn't get anybody to play softball," KT agreed, just as cautiously.

"Then it wasn't all just a dream?" Max asked.

KT realized what a risk he'd taken even mentioning it. If she hadn't remembered, she might have laughed at him, might have screamed at him, might have cursed him out of the room. Even now he was sitting on the edge of his chair, as if he was prepared to bolt if she got upset.

"Evangeline said that other world wasn't real," KT said. "After you . . . left . . . I talked to her again."

"So, were all three of us just dreaming the same dream?" Max asked, squinting in confusion. "Is that even possible?"

"Evangeline would know," KT said confidently. "Got your phone with you? We'll call her."

She meant, *I'll call her*. This at least was something she could take control of.

But Max didn't dig into his pocket for his phone. He looked down at the floor.

"KT, I already tried to call her," Max said. "I looked up her home number. Her dad answered. He was just there stopping by temporarily. I was lucky anyone answered."

KT wondered why Max was telling her all those unnecessary details. Did he want her to congratulate him for showing some initiative on his own? For actually being brave enough to dial a phone and talk to some girl's dad?

Max was still talking.

"Because . . . it turns out . . . Evangeline is a patient in this hospital too," Max said. "She got hurt in an explosion."

"Oh—I knew that!" KT crowed. "She told me in the other world. She said that was how she got there. It was because of a chemistry experiment in her garage, right? Doesn't that prove, well, *something,* that I know that? And I hadn't heard about it for real? How else would—"

"KT, Evangeline hasn't been conscious since the explosion," Max said. "Since last week."

It felt like Max had grabbed her by the shoulders—even the injured one—and shoved her back down against the bed. Why was KT yammering on about proof, when Evangeline was hurt so badly? KT remembered what Evangeline had said she'd been afraid of: *All I ever was, was smart. What if it turns out that I'm not smart anymore, back in the real world?*

What if Evangeline never got up the courage to come back? What would happen to her then?

How much longer could she survive in the fake world?

KT swung her legs over the side of the bed.

"What are you doing?" Max asked.

"We're going to go talk to Evangeline. In person," KT said.

"Weren't you listening?" Max asked. "She's unconscious. She can't tell us anything."

KT looked at her brother.

"But we can tell her what we know," KT said. "Don't you think sometimes smart kids need to be told things too?"

Chapter Twenty-nine

Going to talk to Evangeline turned out to be a little more complicated than KT had expected. There was the matter of the monitor, still hooked up to track KT's every heartbeat. There was the matter of the nurses who ran into the room when KT tried to detach the monitor herself. And, of course, Mom and Dad, running back, still sobbing, and completely unable to understand why KT was insisting on visiting some injured girl they'd never heard her mention before.

"Sweetheart, we are not even allowed to tell you what room that other girl is in," the head nurse said, shaking her beaded braids. "Patient privacy laws, you know? So you just lie still, take it easy."

"Evangeline is in room 3215," Max said. "Right down the hall and in the next corridor."

All the adults turned and stared at him.

"What?" he said. "I've just been paying attention. Can I

help it if you have patients' names written in big letters on your charts over at the nurse's station?"

His eyes met KT's, and she knew he was thinking, *I'm paying attention now. Since I got back from weirdo world.*

"I promise, I won't disturb Evangeline," KT said. "And I won't do anything to . . . exert myself. But I *might* get all upset and stressed out if I can't talk to Evangeline. And couldn't that be dangerous?"

This was world-class manipulation. But the nurses looked at Mom and Dad, and Mom and Dad gave defeated shrugs.

Geez, how sick am I? KT wondered.

She pushed that thought aside and concentrated on shifting into a wheelchair—"just as a precaution," the nurse assured her.

Max pushed her down the hallway, leaving the collection of adults behind.

When they got to Evangeline's room, KT realized she hadn't thought about preparing for the next obstacle. As soon as Max pushed KT across the threshold, Evangeline's parents stood up and moved protectively toward the door: two rumpled, anguished adults who looked like they'd slept in uncomfortable hospital chairs the past three or four nights.

Or maybe they hadn't slept at all for the past three or four nights. Maybe they'd just spent three or four days and nights crying in uncomfortable hospital chairs beside their motionless daughter's bed.

That just means they're defenseless, KT told herself. *Even in a wheelchair, even with a heart condition and a torn rotator cuff, I could brush them aside.*

"Hi!" KT said, pulling a tone of artificial cheer into her

voice. "We're Evangeline's friends from school! We came as soon as we could!"

Evangeline's parents moved in unison, blocking the path toward Evangeline's bed.

"We don't know you," her father said. "We've never seen you before. And—Evangeline told us she didn't have any friends at school."

Not completely defenseless, KT thought. *And . . . not stupid.* She dropped the fake cheer.

"You're right," she said quietly. "Sort of. At the time of the . . . explosion . . . I don't think Evangeline had any friends at school. I'll admit, I wasn't her friend then. But . . . things have changed."

KT saw Evangeline's parents looking at the wheelchair, at the unwieldy brace on KT's arm. Their gaze traveled to Max, and KT glanced back at him as well. For the first time she noticed that he had a bruise on his forehead, and a bandage partially hidden in his hair.

KT realized that Max had shoved his hair back on purpose. He wanted his injuries to show.

Evangeline's father took a step back.

"She's our only child," he said. "She's all we have."

KT realized he was negotiating. Or—giving them a warning. He might as well have said, *You do anything to hurt our daughter, nothing would stop us from retaliating. We have nothing left to lose.*

"The doctors say there is no reason for this," Evangeline's mother, gesturing sadly toward Evangeline's unmoving figure. "They say none of her injuries should keep her from waking. They can't understand."

And I can't understand why you always dressed Evangeline

in those stupid little-girl dresses and second-grade-style pig-tails, KT thought. *Did you ever think you're the reason she was so unpopular? Because you made her look weird? Not because she was so smart?*

But what if dressing her daughter that way had been Evangeline's mother's "thing," the way softball was always KT's thing?

Not anymore, KT thought. Then she pushed the thought aside, because she couldn't handle that right now. Not when she needed to focus on Evangeline.

Evangeline is just going to have to deal with her mother's lack of fashion sense herself, KT thought. *After Max and I get her to come back from the fake alternate world.*

"Could we maybe just talk to Evangeline?" Max asked hesitantly. "Just by ourselves?"

Evangeline's parents looked at each other. Maybe they really did feel like they had nothing left to lose, because they seemed to be considering it.

"The doctor did say it would be good for her to hear other voices," Evangeline's mother said hesitantly. "To know that we're not the only ones who want her to . . . to . . ."

Her eyes filled with tears. What was it with parents who couldn't finish their sentences?

"You can talk to her, but we're not leaving the room," Evangeline's dad said firmly. "We'll be right here."

They moved to the side, letting KT and Max past. But KT could tell Evangeline's parents were going to be straining to hear every single word they said.

"Max, could you fix the strap on this brace?" KT said loudly. "I can't get it one-handed."

"What? You mean—?" Max leaned down to peer at her arm, his face twisted into a confused squint. Which made sense, because KT wasn't even sure there *were* straps on the brace.

As soon as he got close, KT whispered, "I'll talk to Evangeline. You distract her parents."

Max frowned, but after he straightened up, he stepped back toward Evangeline's parents rather than toward the bed.

"My sister and I were really sorry to hear what happened to Evangeline," he said. He sounded so awkward and uncomfortable that KT was sure the grown-ups would see through his act.

No, wait. He's a twelve-year-old boy visiting a girl in her hospital room. Of course he's going to sound awkward and uncomfortable, she told herself. *You go, Max! Keep it up!*

She tuned out the murmured replies from Evangeline's parents and rolled herself closer to the bed. She could see the edge of a plaster cast on Evangeline's leg, sticking out the side of the sheets. But other than that, KT couldn't tell how badly Evangeline had been injured. The girl's dark hair fanned across the pillow, and KT realized this was the first time she'd ever seen Evangeline without her too-tight, too-high twin pigtails.

She didn't even look like Evangeline anymore. She looked like a total stranger.

"Um," KT whispered, leaning close so no one but Evangeline could hear her. "So how's that mathletics club-team tryout working out for you in the other world?"

The girl on the pillow didn't move.

"I don't know how the timing of these things works, but if

you want to finish the tryouts, I wouldn't blame you," KT said, still whispering. "I wouldn't want to interrupt something like that. But you know, once that's over, well, you wouldn't want to get trapped in the other world, would you? I mean, I think I stayed a little too long, and things got kind of scary there at the end. You know we're waiting for you here, don't you? Max and me, we'll be here for you no matter what, all right?"

Evangeline still didn't move.

"You know it's not real, that other world," KT went on. "You're the one who told me about that. Don't you want your life to matter? Don't you want to come out and do great things here in the real world?"

Max cleared his throat behind her. KT whirled around and glared, because didn't he understand that he was supposed to *keep* distracting Evangeline's parents?

"The doctor came in," Max whispered. "Something about test results. I think they're going to be busy for a while."

KT glanced back over her shoulder. Evangeline's parents and a woman in a white coat were bent over a counter near the entrance to the room.

"That's lucky," KT whispered back. "But—I don't think Evangeline hears me."

"Let me try," Max said. He leaned in close and said, "Evangeline? I looked something up. There's this math competition for sixth-, seventh-, and eighth-graders that other schools are part of, not that far away from Brecksville. Maybe you and me and Ben and some other kids, maybe we could talk our school into letting us do that too. It wouldn't be quite like mathletics in the fake world, but it could still be fun. Maybe."

KT stared at her brother.

"You looked that up for Evangeline?" she asked, her eyebrows cocked in amazement. *All right, Max!* she thought. *You're showing initiative all over the place now, aren't you?*

"Well . . . ," Max said, grimacing.

KT realized Max hadn't looked that up for Evangeline. He'd looked it up for himself.

"Still, good for you," KT said, nodding approvingly. "See, Evangeline, see what's possible in the real world?"

Maybe it was only KT's imagination, but Evangeline's face just looked paler than ever. More like a dead person's.

KT reminded herself that Evangeline was terrified that the explosion in the garage had injured her brain somehow—and had maybe even made it so that she wouldn't be smart anymore in the real world. Math competitions weren't the way to entice her back. They would just be a cruel reminder of what she'd lost.

But *had* Evangeline actually injured her brain?

KT realized she didn't know.

Did it matter? If Evangeline had lost some of her brilliance, wouldn't it still be worth it for her to come back?

KT glanced back at the grown-ups. Still talking. Still distracted. There was still time.

"Evangeline," KT said, and she choked a little on the last syllable. "There was bad news waiting for me when I got back to the real world. I've got some sort of heart condition I never knew about before—I'm not sure I'll ever be able to play softball again. Not for real. Not competitively. Not the way I want to." Her throat ached, and for a minute KT thought she was going to break down sobbing. But she swallowed hard and kept going.

"But there was good news too," she went on. "One part of

the good news was, the thing I was most afraid of—that I'd really hurt Max when I hit him with that softball—that wasn't true. I got all terrified about that for nothing."

KT heard Max make a startled noise beside her, but she didn't turn to look at him again. She couldn't. Instead she grabbed Evangeline's hand and went on.

"And the other good news was—and I'm still kind of figuring this out—the good news was, I could stand the bad news," KT said. "Being told I couldn't play softball—last week I would have thought that that would be unbearable, the worst news possible. But it wasn't. I would have thought it would kill me. But it didn't. I'm still here. I'm still me. And—I'm okay. I don't know how, but I'm going to beat this thing. And you're going to beat your problems, too!"

She jerked Evangeline's hand up and down, pounding it against the sheets.

"You and me, we *are* alike!" she told Evangeline. "We're winners! We're going to come out on top!"

Max leaned forward and pulled KT's arm back, pulling her away from Evangeline.

"Quit it, KT," he complained. "You sound like a coach."

"Why do you have to make that sound like a bad thing?" KT asked.

"Because," Max said. He gulped a little. "Because sometimes people lose."

There was a hollowness in his voice that KT had never heard before. She didn't know if he'd been hiding it before, or if she just hadn't been paying attention.

"But if they really try—," KT began.

"Do you know how hard I tried in T-ball?" Max asked. "Dad

would say, 'Just hit the ball, Max-Max!' And I'd swing, and it'd be like there was a hole that suddenly appeared in the bat, or the ball jumped out of the way . . . I swear, I was trying my absolute hardest, but I couldn't hit that ball!"

KT kind of remembered this: Max had been spectacularly bad at T-ball.

"Maybe you were just a little too young," KT said apologetically. "Maybe—"

"It doesn't matter now," Max said, shrugging. "Never mind. *I* don't care anymore."

"So why'd you bring it up?" KT challenged.

She could almost see Max forcing himself not to back away.

"Because," he said in an even voice, "you're used to winning, so you don't even think about how, every time there's a game, both sides get that 'rah, rah, team' speech from their coaches. Both sides hear, 'You're the best!' 'You've got to win!' 'You're the greatest!' But half of the people playing that game are going to walk away losers. Half!"

Max was right. KT was used to winning. So she hadn't ever thought of sports that way.

"In something like a race, *most* of the people are going to lose," Max went on. "Say there's ten people running—ninety percent of them will lose!"

KT felt a new kind of fear grip her heart. Her mind made an appalling leap. What if he wasn't really talking about races? What if he was working up to some sort of terrifying comparison?

"What do you mean?" she asked. Now it was her turn to grab Max's arm. "Did you hear some sort of stat from Mom and Dad, about how many people recover from this heart thing I've got? Listen, even if it's only ten percent of people who get to go back to playing sports, I'm going to be in that ten percent!"

Max jerked his arm away.

"I don't know anything more than you do about your heart thing," Max said. There was fear in his voice too. "I was talking about Evangeline."

"Since when does Evangeline have anything to do with sports?" KT demanded.

"If you'd let me finish . . . ," Max said, rolling his eyes. "I was trying to make a point. People act like other things at school are sports too. Like, for some kids to 'win' at being popular, other kids have to lose. If someone wants to be cool, they get that way by making fun of kids who aren't cool. So . . . even nerds like me used to make fun of Evangeline. We put her down to build ourselves up."

"You think you can convince Evangeline to come back by telling her you used to make fun of her?" KT asked incredulously.

"No. To get her to understand how much things can change," Max said quietly. "How much *I* want to change things. Did you ever think that maybe it wasn't just a mistake, Evangeline blowing up her garage? Did you ever think that things might have been so bad for her that . . . that she did it on purpose?"

KT reeled backward. She hadn't thought of that. She was actually glad that she had the wheelchair underneath and behind her. And, anyhow, Max put a steadying arm on her shoulder. He was there to hold her up too, if she needed him.

KT grabbed Evangeline's arm once more.

"Evangeline, please," she said. "I promise you, things will

be different if you come back. *When* you come back. No matter what happens with your injuries, no matter what happens with my heart problems—we're a team now. Everything's better when you've got a team around you. You, me, Max— we'll show those other kids different ways to be winners!"

Dimly KT realized that trying so hard to wake up Evangeline was partly just a way to avoid thinking about her own problems.

But what's wrong with that? she wondered. *Isn't it better to do something good for someone else, rather than obsess about myself? Or—hide from everything in some fake alternate world?*

This didn't feel like hiding. This felt more like . . . like growing past her own problems. Like finding a new way to win.

"Please, Evangeline!" she repeated.

She was practically screaming now. Well, who cared if Evangeline's parents and the doctor heard that last part? Who cared if the whole hospital heard? She had to make her voice loud enough to drown out the echo of Max's voice in her head: *Sometimes people lose.* KT knew it was possible that Evangeline would never wake up. It was possible that she would die. It was possible that KT's heart would never heal enough that she could play softball again. It was possible that KT would die.

Was it also possible that Evangeline's eyelids were starting to flutter open? Or did KT just think that because she wanted it to happen so badly? Because she always, always, always wanted her team to win?

Epil0gue

→ Three and a half years later

It was the first day of school at Brecksville Middle School North. The new sixth graders, looking young and scared and barely hatched from elementary school, sat waiting in the auditorium. They'd already spent most of the morning being told how to open their lockers, how to organize their plan books, and how to find their way around the school. Now, Principal Arnold announced, some students from the high school were going to talk to them.

Striding toward the podium, KT scanned the faces in the crowd. She thought that maybe some of the kids had perked up at the mention of high schoolers. She hoped they had—she wanted them to actually listen.

"The young lady you're about to hear from is a very involved, very busy student over at the high school," Mr. Arnold said. "It's KT Sutton—KT, you want to remind me what all you're doing? Are you playing any sports?"

This was a scripted question—she'd asked Mr. Arnold to

ask her this. But for a moment it took her breath away, the cruelty of it all. The cruelty of her life.

"No, Mr. Arnold, I don't play any sports," she said. "For some reason the high school's a little cowardly about putting athletes out on the field when they have a good chance of keeling over dead if they run to catch a ball."

Mr. Arnold winced—she hadn't exactly warned him about her answer. She recognized the look in his eye: He would want to have a little talk with her afterward. But she was a high-school senior now. She wasn't afraid of the middle-school principal.

And anyhow, her blunt words had accomplished what she wanted. The entire auditorium had fallen silent. The boys in the back rows had stopped fidgeting in their seats. The girls who looked like they'd spent the whole summer figuring out what to wear the first day had stopped messing around with each other's hair.

Everyone was listening now.

"So, sixth grade," KT said speculatively. "I remember the first day of my sixth-grade year. I thought I had middle school all figured out. I remember, I sat right there." She pointed out into the crowd, toward a section just a few rows from the back. Appropriately enough, the group of kids sitting there now looked like they might be athletes. "I thought I was going to be the greatest softball player Brecksville North had ever seen. And then I was going to be the greatest softball player Brecksville High had ever seen. And, after that, I was planning to get a softball scholarship to college and become the greatest softball player the whole *world* had ever seen."

"So what happened?" a kid called out. He probably thought

that was his bid for the role of class clown. Out of the corner of her eye KT saw Mr. Arnold narrow his eyes and write something down on a clipboard.

KT didn't care.

"What happened?" she repeated. "Real life. Sixth grade did go the way I expected it to. So did seventh. But then, during a softball game my eighth-grade year, I collapsed on the field and found out I had a heart problem I'd never known about. I could have died because of it. I was lucky I didn't."

It had been a long time before her parents had explained exactly how bad things had looked for KT on the field of the Rysdale Invitational finals. She'd been lucky her collapse had actually just been from fainting, not anything worse. But she'd also been lucky that one of the parents of the Cobras was a cardiologist who'd insisted that she be checked for something called hypertrophic cardiomyopathy.

It was just unlucky that she actually had it.

"Even then," KT went on, "even being told sports could kill me, I kept thinking, *Well, I'll surprise everyone and heal completely. I'll be the one person who recovers and goes back to being a star athlete.* But I didn't. I can't. Sure, the doctors tell me I can have a normal life, but only if my normal life doesn't include playing my favorite sport."

The sixth graders looked appropriately horrified, so she didn't add any extra information about all the tests she'd had, all the time she'd spent in medical facilities, all the discussions she'd been in about treatment options . . . She didn't tell them how hard she'd cried the first time someone told her some competitive sports were allowed—but only "sports" like billiards and archery. Three years of high school had already

slipped by, and she'd been benched from softball the whole time. She now understood that she probably would be the rest of her life.

And yet . . .

"But you know what?" KT said. "It's okay. I've found other things to get involved with. A variety of groups: service clubs and artsy clubs and even a few things connected to academics. I've made friends I wouldn't have had otherwise. I'm busy. I'm happy. I'm fine."

Two years ago, the first time KT had come back to speak at the middle school, it had been hard to say these words. They hadn't quite sounded true. This time KT was surprised at how easily that "I'm happy" slipped off her tongue.

If I got zapped into some sort of alternate world where I could have played softball all through high school, would I actually have wanted to? she wondered. *Or would I just think about everything else that I wouldn't get to do? The challenging classes that turned out to be fun, that I wouldn't have taken because they would have interfered with softball. The friends I never would have made, or even bothered to speak to: Miguel from drama club, Ally from service club, Teddy and Misha and Stu from the Special Olympics team I've been coaching, and of course my best friend, who . . .*

KT got distracted, because one of the girls in the front row was making a snarky comment in a slightly too loud voice.

"Oh, *I* know what this is about," the girl said in a bored, haughty tone. "This is one of those stupid 'when life gives you lemons, make lemonade' speeches."

She rolled her eyes, and the girls on either side of her quickly adjusted their own expressions to imitate her smirk.

KT fixed the girl with the same kind of deadeye stare she'd once used on opposing batters.

Sorry, kiddo, I know you're only a sixth grader, she thought. *But you just made yourself fair game.*

"No, girl in the front row, this is not a 'when life gives you lemons, make lemonade' speech," KT countered. "This is a 'no matter what life gives you, don't treat the people around you like lemons' speech."

The front-row girl—and both of her sidekicks—looked totally confused.

"You're all starting middle school," KT said. "And maybe you're sitting there thinking you know exactly who you are and what you're good at and how you're going to fit in here at Brecksville North. Or maybe you don't have a clue. Either way, you probably think you can look around and know those things about the other kids. You've probably already started labeling the other kids popular or outcast or hot or ugly or smart or stupid or talented or useless or someone you would want for a friend or someone you would never in a million years be friends with. But you know what? You don't know anything at all about the people around you."

Snarky girl in the front row looked like she wanted to keep making nasty comments, but she was afraid that she might miss something if she did.

"This is *middle* school," KT continued. "All of you are going to change a lot in the next three years. A jock like me might end up benched. The so-called popular kids may be the ones everyone hates by Christmas. The ugliest kid in the school might end up being the hottest guy in your class by eighth grade."

KT instantly regretted saying that last part, because half the auditorium turned to peer at one particular kid. He looked like his hair had never met a brush or a comb, and his ears and mouth and nose seemed to have reached grown-up size about five years before the rest of him. But he just sat up straight and looked back at the others with something like confidence, as if to say, *Oh, yeah? Hear that? Whatever you think of me now, I might be hot by eighth grade!*

"But, believe me, you are really going to miss out over the next three years if all you see when you look at your fellow classmates are labels," KT went on. "You're going to miss out on finding out what makes them interesting, and they're going to miss out on finding out what makes you interesting."

It was almost time for KT's sales job.

"That's why some other high-school kids and I started a club for middle schoolers a few years ago," KT said. "A club where kids can talk about anything they want to. Where they can share what they're thinking without being labeled weird. We voted to call it the Evangeline club."

As KT could have predicted, snarky girl in the first row whirled around to her friends and said in a voice loud enough for KT to hear, "Sounds like a club for losers! I would never join that!"

KT needed to bring out her secret weapons.

"Let me introduce a few other kids involved with the group to help me explain," KT said. "Max? Ben?"

Her brother and his best friend stepped out from behind the stage curtain. A stunned hush fell over the crowd, followed by a rush of high-pitched, sixth-grade-girl whispers. Even snark-girl in the front row immediately hissed to her friends, "Let's join that club! I don't care what we have to do, I want to meet those guys!"

Max and Ben had both gone through an incredible meta-morphosis over the past three and a half years. Max was still KT's brother, and Ben might as well have been, so she still tended to think of them as just a couple of goofy guys. But other girls drooled over them all the time now.

Is it that Max is actually that good-looking, or do girls just think that because he acts so confident now? KT wondered. *And . . . he's managed to keep Ben from being a total jerk about his looks, so everyone likes both of them?*

Whatever. They were having the right effect on the sixth graders.

Ben leaned toward the microphone and said in his now-deep, cool-sounding voice, "The whole time I was in middle school, I was terrified that someone might find out that my real first name was Ebenezer. If we'd had an Evangeline club back then, I could have just told everyone in the group, and that would have been that. My terror would have ended three years early."

KT could practically see half the guys in the audience think-ing, *Whoa. I wish my real first name was Ebenezer. Then people would think I was cool.* And many of the girls seemed to be thinking, *Ebenezer. What a great name. I'm going to name my first kid that. After I marry this guy, of course.*

The nerdy name had been transformed just because some-one who looked like Ben admitted that it was his.

Max took his turn at the microphone.

"And when I was in middle school, I had my parents nag-ging me and nagging me to join a sports team, to get some exercise, to do *something*," he said. "And I was too embarrassed to tell them that there was actually a sport that I kind of liked, and would be willing to try."

Ben rested his arm on Max's shoulder in that casual way guy jocks always had.

"You are looking at the cocaptains of the Brecksville High School bowling team," he drawled into the microphone.

The entire auditorium full of sixth graders laughed and cheered. In that moment they seemed to forget that the only cool sports for boys were football and basketball and baseball. It was like they were all vowing to become bowling fans.

Well, Mom and Dad adapted, KT thought, grinning a little to herself.

She was actually kind of proud of the way her parents had become the biggest boosters the bowling team had. At least they still had *some* sporting event to watch one of their kids play. It was a nice distraction from all of KT's heart problems. And the heart problems did keep Mom and Dad from forcing KT to go watch Max play, too. But sometimes she went to cheer her brother on anyway.

"Oh, we're on math team too!" Ben added, and the auditorium roared again, probably because the sixth graders thought it was a joke.

We'll let them come to the first Evangeline club meeting before we tell them that's true, KT thought.

"We're making this sound like it's all fun and games, because, well, we're kind of funny guys," Max said with a shrug that KT thought was sure to endear him even more to the audience. "But the Evangeline club does serve a serious purpose."

This was KT's cue to step back to the microphone.

"Back when the three of us were in middle school, one of our fellow students, Evangeline, had a tough time of it," KT began. "She was—well, there's no other word for it—weird. She wore clothes nobody else would be caught dead in, and she thought about things nobody else thought about, and she told the teachers they needed to make their homework assignments harder."

Someone in the back of the auditorium began booing.

"Yeah, that's what I thought too," KT said, nodding. "But it gets worse. She sent an e-mail to all the administrators and coaches and teachers and everybody telling them that they should get rid of school sports and spend all their time and energy on school itself."

The booing got louder.

KT held up her hand to silence it.

"Now, you can probably guess that I didn't agree with that myself," she said, rolling her eyes for emphasis. "But Evangeline was entitled to her opinion. And there were other kids who actually felt the same way she did. Who maybe could have teamed up with her and had fun together. Built up some new groups at the school for themselves, instead of trying to take away the things that other kids thought were fun."

Now Max leaned toward the microphone.

"But for kids like me, the last thing we wanted was to have someone think we were friends with Evangeline. What if people decided that made us as weird as her?" he asked, and in just that moment, he sounded like his sixth-grade self again: forlorn and cowardly.

KT realized that the auditorium had fallen silent once more.

"So Evangeline didn't have any friends," KT continued. "After that e-mail a lot of the adults were mad at her too. She couldn't see an end to it. And so this brilliant, talented kid started doing things to mess up her own life. She had all these opportunities ahead of her, if she could just stick it out through middle school. But she was ready to throw it all away."

KT's voice had taken on a huskiness that flowed out into the quiet room, seeming to affect the new, unformed sixth graders more than she'd expected. Somehow it was different kids she picked out in the crowd now. Amid the jocks and the nerds and the brainiacs and the queen-bee wannabes, certain faces were wrinkled up in concern, as if the kids behind the faces were thinking, *I would have been her friend. I would have talked to her, no matter what other people thought of me.*

And, just as she had the past two years, giving this same speech, KT reminded herself, *See? Even in middle school there are some kids who are truly kind.*

She really needed to get some of those kids into this year's Evangeline club, or it would never work.

But a wave of whispers was also starting to cross the room, gossipy mutterings that KT caught in bits and pieces:

"Was there some girl three or four years ago who actually committed *suicide*?"

"How is it our fault if some girl offed herself because she didn't have any friends?"

"What are we supposed to do about something that happened so long ago?"

KT let the whispers reach their crest, then she leaned back toward the microphone.

"But you don't just have to take my word for all of this," KT said. "Why don't we let Evangeline tell her own story?"

The sixth graders let out a collective gasp. The curtains at the side of the auditorium began to sway, and all the kids in the room snapped their attention in that direction.

Slowly, dramatically, Evangeline stepped out from behind the curtain.

"Yep, that's me!" she announced, her voice loud enough to carry through the room without amplification. She posed, a hand on her hip. "Ta-da!"

All the sixth graders burst out laughing—laughing with Evangeline, not at her. KT almost expected them to break out chanting like the cheerleaders back in weirdo world: "E, E-V, E-V-A-N-G-E-L, and I-N-E!"

For Evangeline had changed just as much as Max and Ben in the past three years. It wasn't that she'd turned beautiful—*well,* KT thought, studying the other girl's face, *maybe she could be beautiful if she wanted to, but she'd think that was way too boring and ordinary.* Instead she'd become cool. Where her odd clothes had seemed pathetic and weird in middle school, now they gave her an air of being more stylish than anyone else, in a funky, hippie-chick kind of way. The thrift-store paisley skirt she was wearing now made all the Abercrombie and Hollister clones in the audience look cookie-cutter dull.

Evangeline flipped back her two long pigtails—worn stylishly low now, not little-girl high, which could almost count as a concession to fashion. Or maybe it was just easier, and the style was a sign that she had more important things to think about than hair.

She turned and began walking toward the podium.

Step-slide, step-slide, step-slide . . .

Evangeline still had a slight limp left over from the explosion three years ago. She always insisted it didn't actually matter: "I was never going to be a great athlete, anyhow. It was my brain I was worried about, remember? And that's still working fine."

That was always the cue for KT or Max to say, "Or at least no more scrambled and weird than usual."

Evangeline was maybe exaggerating the limp a little today, for effect. The laughing sixth graders settled down, and the compassionate-faced ones started looking worried again.

Evangeline got to the microphone at the podium, and KT, Max, and Ben took a few steps back to give her room.

"KT always likes to make my story sound extreme, and it could have gotten truly awful if I hadn't eventually found her and Max as friends," Evangeline said. "But the only bad thing I really did on purpose was flunk a math test. Blowing up my parents' garage—that was completely accidental! Honest!"

The sixth graders burst into laughter once again, and under the cover of the crowd noise KT muttered, "That wasn't what I was talking about and you know it."

And, while the laughter continued, Evangeline muttered back, "Yeah, but how could we explain what really happened? Oh wait, I know . . ."

As the laughter subsided, Evangeline leaned back into the microphone and proclaimed, "For me, middle school was a lot like being zapped into an alternate world!"

The sixth graders laughed again. It was like this was the most fun they'd had all day. KT moved farther away from the spotlight, offstage, because Evangeline was going to be talking for a while now.

KT realized she'd ended up standing right beside Principal Arnold. Oh, well. She'd just have to keep him distracted.

"Why is it," she whispered, "that when Evangeline was in middle school, all the kids hated her for being so quirky and offbeat and weird? And now that's what middle-school kids love about her?"

"She's not their age," Mr. Arnold whispered back. "So she's not as threatening. And—she's not desperate for friends anymore. She's not desperate for anything. She gives them hope for what they could become if they want to be quirky and offbeat and weird themselves."

"Makes sense, I guess," KT muttered.

"While we're talking . . . ," Mr. Arnold began.

Uh-oh. So much for KT's distraction techniques.

"You're graduating this year, right?" Mr. Arnold continued. "Have you figured out what you want to study in college? Not that you have to decide everything right now, but—please tell me middle-school guidance counselor is on your list of possible careers."

"What?" KT was floored. "Me? A *guidance counselor*?"

"Sure," Mr. Arnold said. "You've done so well with the Evangeline club, and—"

"Oh, no," KT shook her head fiercely. "That's been all of us working together, and, well, you know. We only had three kids in the club the first year. And seven last year. And . . ."

"And for those three and seven kids, didn't it make a huge difference?" Mr. Arnold asked. "And don't you think there's a ripple effect with the attitudes in the school as a whole?"

"But—I was just nasty to one of the girls in the crowd. I couldn't work very well with kids like that," KT complained. "And I talked about keeling over dead! And you *glared* at me!"

"Don't you think principals can play things for effect sometimes too?" Mr. Arnold asked, with a wink.

Was he just messing with her mind?

KT decided she had to tell him the truth, regardless.

"Actually," she said, "I was thinking I'd go to med school someday. To figure out how kids like me can be cured."

"Ah," Mr. Arnold said, with a shrug. "That's a good goal too. Just think about what I said, because you've got a lot of different talents you might want to develop."

A lot of different talents . . . How could that be when KT had once thought she wasn't good at anything but softball?

"I'm not just thinking about my own problems," KT said, a little defensively. "It's just that I still think like an athlete, even if I can't play anymore. I need to have an opponent. This heart thing—I want to be able to fight it."

"Fair enough," Mr. Arnold said. "But don't you like fighting ignorance and cruelty, too?"

She did. KT had loved every minute of organizing the Evangeline clubs.

"Well," she said grudgingly, "let me see how I do in AP chemistry this year. It may be that I'm not even good enough at science to ever be a doctor."

"Chemistry?" Mr. Arnold said. "I *loved* chemistry when I was in school. You need any help, come talk to me."

As had happened so often over the past three years, KT had a sudden flash of connection with the alternate world.

Mr. Arnold was a former chemademics star there, she remembered.

Was it possible that the alternate world had not been quite as far-fetched as it had seemed? Was it possible that the real world contained all sorts of hidden alternate worlds within its boundaries—and that real people did too?

In the past three years Evangeline had come up with all sorts of theories and hypotheses to explain the alternate world and exactly how she, KT, and Max could possibly have all imagined the same thing at once. She'd even had a paper published in an obscure psychology journal that probably only ten people in the whole world bothered to read. KT had barely been able to make it through the title—something about "shared consciousnesses in an altered fugue state." But then, KT didn't actually care about explanations. It was enough for her to know that when the real world had become too painful to face, they'd all been able to escape to another world.

And, with one another's help, they'd all managed to return safely, in time, with new ways to cope.

"Listen to that," Mr. Arnold said, clapping KT on the back. "Evangeline's getting even more applause than she did last year."

KT realized that Evangeline was done talking now. KT hadn't been listening, but she knew that Evangeline would have given a somewhat fictionalized account of being in a coma for three days and coming out of it only when she heard Max and KT begging for her return.

Now Evangeline was dipping down into an exaggerated curtsy that somehow made fun of curtsies and looked incredibly graceful, all at once. Mr. Arnold moved past her, clapping along with the students.

"Isn't it great to see how Brecksville North students grow up?" Mr. Arnold said into the microphone.

And he's playing that for effect too, KT realized. *He's trying to sound nerdy and uncool! Because . . . he doesn't actually want to sound too proud of us?*

Evangeline stepped back and stood between KT and Max. She draped her arms over both their shoulders.

"Thank you," she said, so softly that only they could hear.

"For what?" KT said.

"You know," Evangeline said. "Saving me. If I hadn't heard you two calling for me, I would have stayed in the alternate world too long. It would have collapsed on me, and I would have died."

"That's only a theory," KT said, then added jokingly, "It's not very scientific of you to treat it as fact."

"I know what I know," Evangeline said. "You did save me."

KT nodded, accepting this. She gave Evangeline a very jocklike punch on the arm.

"Works both ways," she said. "I don't think I would have gotten out safely either, if you hadn't told me what was going to happen."

"Teams work together," Evangeline said, shrugging.

"And sometimes they actually do win," Max said.

"And sometimes they can't help but lose," Evangeline said.

KT pressed her hand over her chest, where her infuriatingly defective heart thumped on—broken, but somehow still beating steadily and well. She hugged her best friend close.

"And sometimes," KT countered, "that's not even what matters most."

+ AUTHOR'S NOTE +

Hypertrophic cardiomyopathy, the condition that ended KT's softball career, is a disorder involving an abnormally thick heart muscle. Usually hereditary, it can go undetected for years. Although it can cause symptoms such as chest pains, dizziness, and fainting, in some cases the first sign of the condition is a sudden, seemingly inexplicable collapse and death. Some doctors have called for all young athletes to be screened for hypertrophic cardiomyopathy and other potentially deadly heart issues. Others who are concerned about the problem have focused on trying to ensure that automatic external defibrillators are available at schools and near sports complexes.

With treatment, most hypertrophic cardiomyopathy patients can lead normal lives. But typically, like KT, they are told to avoid intense competitive sports.

ACKNOWLEDGMENTS

Some books arrive so confident and sure of themselves that even I as the author hardly feel right taking much credit for them. Other books seem to require numerous helpers to spark, shape, inspire, influence, and encourage them into being. *Game Changer* was definitely one of those "It takes a village" books.

First of all, I need to thank my family and many friends, librarians, and teachers for cheering on this book even when I wasn't sure how it would work. My agent, Tracey Adams, showed great patience in listening to me rant about the issues I wanted to explore, even when she would have had a good excuse not to. She definitely went above and beyond, helping with this book. I owe my editor, David Gale, for his comments and questions about various drafts of this book—they absolutely made this a much better book. Several friends also read portions of the book in various stages, and I was grateful to get their opinions about both what worked and what didn't: Thanks to Linda Gerber, Erin MacLellan, Jenny Patton, Nancy Roe Pimm, and Linda Stanek.

My neighbors, Dan, Lori, and Mackenzie Nelsen were very generous in sharing information with me about their own softball experiences, and the way they've managed to keep their sanity through it all. They are great neighbors for a multitude of reasons. My daughter, Meredith, was working as my assistant during part of the time I was writing the book, and so she helped with some research as well. I was also quite

ACKNOWLEDGMENTS

fortunate in getting expert help with the medical information needed for this book: Both Dr. William T. Abraham, Director of the Division of Cardiovascular Medicine at The Ohio State University, and Dr. Aaron L. Baggish, Associate Director of the Cardiovascular Performance Program at the Massachusetts General Hospital Heart Center, were kind enough to take time to answer my questions about hypertrophic cardiomyopathy.